A Hand of Father

Justice #7

SUZAN HARDEN

This is a work of fiction. All characters, organizations and events in this novel are products of the author's imagination and are not to be construed as real. Any resemblance to persons, living or dead, is entirely coincidental.

A HAND OF FATHER
(Justice #7)
ISBN-13 - 978-1-938745-95-9
Copyright 2021 by Suzan Harden

Published by Angry Sheep Publishing
Findlay, Ohio

Cover Design by For the Muse Designs
Interior Design by JW Manus

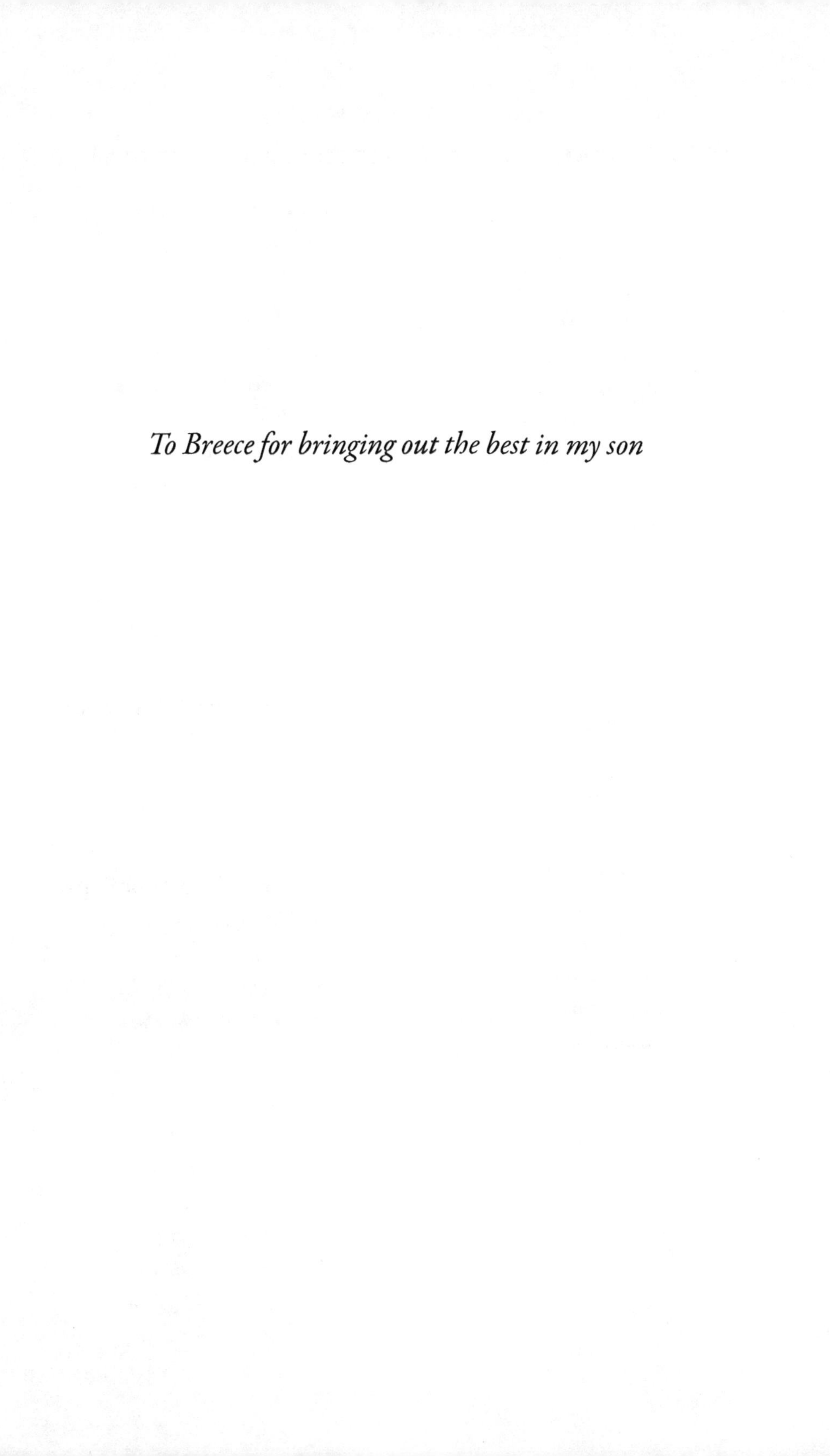

To Breece for bringing out the best in my son

Justice
(the novels)

Justice: The Beginning
A Question of Balance
A Modicum of Truth
A Matter of Death
A Touch of Mother
A Twist of Love
A Virtue of Child
A Hand of Father
A Measure of Knowledge

The Justice Thalia Stories

Snowfall

Murder Most Fowl

The Sweetest Poison

A Granddaughter of Mine

More Stories

Sword and Sorceress 28 ("Justice")

Sword and Sorceress 30 ("Diplomacy in the Dark")

For updates, news, and giveaways, join Suzan's mailing list or visit her website at www.suzanharden.com. You can also check her out on Twitter @Suzan_Harden or on Facebook at SuzanHardenWriter.

Prologue

Father was working at His forge when Child came to Him for assistance. He smiled and laid aside His hammer and tongs.

"What may I do for You, My Daughter?"

"I have damaged My plow, Father." She held up the broken shards of metal. "I wanted to prepare a new field to plant corn and beans. While My oxen dragged the plow, the blade struck a large rock in the middle of the meadow, and the steel cracked."

Father frowned as He examined the metal. "I can repair it, My Daughter. But if You try to plow where the rock sits, the blade will merely break again."

"I shall heed your wisdom, Father, and remove the rock." Child bowed and left Her blade to be mended. She returned to the meadow. She began digging around the rock, but She could not find the bottom edge.

Her Brother Wildling in the form of a wolf trotted by the meadow. Upon seeing His Sister digging, He approached and asked, "What are You doing?"

Child explained Her predicament, to which Wildling responded, "Digging looks like fun! Let Me help You."

Together the Two dug until They could not see the sun. Yet, They still had not found the bottom of the rock.

Wildling became bored with the game. "Let Us forget about the rock.

It is a hot day. A cool swim would remove the dirt from My fur and Your skin."

But the rock vexed Child, and She would not give up. Wildling shook His head at His Sister's stubbornness and trotted to a lake to wash off the soil embedded in His coat.

Child then visited Mother who said to ask Father. So Child went to the Others. Knowledge made the same suggestion of asking Father. Thief laughed at Child and told Her to find another place for Her corn and beans.

Light suggested adding more soil to the meadow so Her plants would have more room for their roots overtop of the rock. Vintner wanted Her to relinquish Her quest and spend the afternoon drinking mead with Him.

Love wondered if the rock was a diamond. When Child said it was a plain old rock, just very big and in the middle of Her planned field, Love suggested talking to Conflict. He followed Her to the meadow and struck the rock with His massive hammer. While the hammer did not break, it only chipped off a few pebbles from the rock with each blow.

Child thanked Conflict for His efforts, which gave Her an idea. She traveled to Death, and once again explained Her situation. "Can you kill the rock for me?

"I cannot take anything before its time, My Dear," Death said softly. "And when the rock has crumbled to dust, Your meadow will at the bottom of a new sea and unfit to grow Your crops."

Finally, Child came to Balance. She explained the situation with the rock and asked Balance for Her advice.

"Why don't You plow around the rock instead of trying to move it?" Balance asked.

Perturbed by Balance's question, Child returned to Father. "The other Nine have tried to help Me with the rock to no effect. Instead of helping Me, Balance asked a foolish question."

"What did She say, My Daughter?"

Child repeated the question. And Father chuckled.

"Why are You laughing?" Child cried.

"I also told you not to plow where the rock is. You told Me My advice was wise. Yet, You were the One Who decided to remove the rock." Father shook His head. "But when Balance gives You the exact same advice, You became irritated with Her."

"But I—" Child dropped Her head. He was right. "Forgive me, Father. I should have listened to You more closely."

He hugged Her. "When one cannot go through an obstacle, they must go around. That is true even for Us."

– The Eighth Book of Father, Verses I thru XXIV

Chapter 1

The eleven other seats didn't release me from Child's chains until after the Autumn Equinox. Part of it was concern for what I might do to others, for the dead demons that comprised the grimoire I'd kept had dug their psychic claws deep into my mind. Part of it was worry of what I might do to myself out of shame.

For believing myself immune to the demons' influence.

I was under no illusion my fellow seats cared about my well-being. The demons targeted me because I was the only human who could see them regardless of the form they took.

My sight was different than other humans, thanks again to my arrogance. Like all other female children who were born blind, I was taken to the Temple of Balance in my home nation of Issura. The ancients thought those like me were touched by Balance Herself. In reality, my blindness was a result of my birth mother's attempt to illegally abort me.

However, I assumed if I could restore my sight, I would no longer be bound to the Temple of Balance. But how could I give myself something of which I had no real concept? Instead, I gave myself a form of sight based on the heat an object. Fire blinds me as equally as snow and ice. And I was still bound to Balance because there were things I couldn't see, such as ink on parchment.

But I could always see demons because they were a black far darker than the night sky on a moonless night regardless of any form they took or any illusion they cast. Therefore, I was valuable to my fellow humans in their war against the demons.

Though the demons had tried to take over me, body and spirit, I made it easy for them. I let my pride in my abilities get in the way. A fault High Brother Luc of Light had gently chided me about during the ten years we spent on circuit through the eastern portion of the Duchy of Orrin.

Then there was the guilt of letting the demons use me to abuse my squire Nathan.

While I was imprisoned in Child, there was simply no lying to myself in the presence of High Sister Mya. I would have preferred a truthspell, but as she pointed out, one can only lie if they consciously know the truth they are hiding. There were far more layers to the human mind than most people realized.

The odd thing was Mya simply came down to my cell in the Temple of Child and talked. No magic. No silent speech. No touching of my mind. We just talked.

Also, I couldn't truly call it a cell. Unlike the stone cells beneath Balance for those accused of wrongdoing, the walls and floor where I was kept in Child were covered in oiled leather and padded with horse hair. I had a cotton and linen pallet to sleep upon at night. Even the door was padded.

It was for the protection of those who were mentally ill and had a predilection for self-injury or were a danger to their fellow humans. Otherwise, I would have been kept in one of the treatment rooms on the second floor of the Temple of Child.

"I wish I hadn't ordered the entrances to the tunnel closed," I said one day. Or night. I wasn't quite sure of time anymore with the spell threaded shackles.

Mya looked at me with her sad half-smile. "Why is that?"

"So the Miners Guild could bury me in them," I said. "It's what I deserve."

"Self-pity, again?" The slim, blue brow over her right eye rose.

"No." I played with a fold of the shift I wore. "Embarrassment." I shook my head. "After the lecture I delivered to the mob from the South Side this summer, how can anyone take me seriously as a justice again after what I've done?"

"Do you want to resume being a justice?"

I snorted. "Are you going to tell me I have a choice?" When she remained quiet, I added, "I thought you said we weren't supposed to lie to each other."

"You're right," she murmured. "It would be a lie to say you would be relieved of your duties, but the whole point of these sessions is to evaluate when you're ready to resume your position."

Then she surprised me. "How do you feel about a visitor this afternoon?"

I leaned against the padded leather on the wall. "Who?"

"You don't like surprises do you?" Mya teased.

"No, not really." Even I had to smile. "Surprises in my life have a tendency to want to kill me."

"It's Ming Wei," she admitted. "It's a test for both of you."

I shuddered. Ming Wei was Justice Yanaba's squire as Nathan was mine. She had stopped me from striking the boy. Her desperation to save her friend had unlocked her abilities. She not only saved Nathan's life, but she saved mine as well.

Ming Wei's psychic self showed the woman she should become if she could let go of her emotional pain. The girl had been sold by her parents to a Jing noble who sorely abused her. When his foul deeds were discovered, he burned his manse with himself and his child slaves inside. Ming Wei had been the sole survivor.

"Are you sure that's a good idea for her sake?" I murmured.

"Why don't you want to see her?" Mya asked in return.

"Answering a question with another question got old when I was a novice at the home Temple," I muttered.

Mya chuckled. "And you avoid my questions because you don't like it when you feel out of control."

"The last time I saw her I wasn't in control," I said softly. "Not of myself anyway. Ming Wei has had so much happen to her in her short life. I added to her pain, and-and—" I took another shuddering breath. "I don't know if I can face her after what I did."

"The thing is you didn't strike Nathan." Mya cocked her head. "And if the demons had full control over you . . ."

I finished the ugly thought. "I would have killed Ming Wei, too." I stared at Mya. "Let's discuss the subject we've been dancing around. Why hasn't Yanaba or Elizabeth taken my head?"

"No one really knows what happened at Balance other than the Orrin seats and your staff." Mya shook her head. "I've never seen such personal loyalty to any seat, much less a chief justice."

My short bark of laughter made her jump. "They had to deal with Penelope. Compared to her, I'm a sweetcake at the Winter Solstice." Still, Mya's comment touched my heart.

"After we had a convocation concerning what to do about you, all the seats as well as acting Chief Justice Yanaba decided to see how things went with your treatment here." Mya shrugged. "Elizabeth agreed."

"Though she has no standing in Orrin?" I asked.

"She knows what it's like to be manipulated and tortured, Anthea," Mya said. "Out of everyone in the duchy, she's the most sympathetic to your condition. You gave her a chance to recover and deal with what was done to her. She was your staunchest advocate other than Luc and Claudia."

I asked the question I'd been dreading the most. "And what's the

Reverend Mother of Balance say about all of this?" I gestured to indicate my cell and Mya.

"She doesn't know."

Someone could have knocked me over with a dandelion puff. "No one's told her?"

"The official story is you had a breakdown in your guilt over the death of Claudia's babe at Gerd's hands. You voluntarily and temporarily abdicated your seat to seek treatment because you felt you could no longer perform as an objective jurist."

I blinked a few times as I tried to swallow this information. Yanaba and Elizabeth had threatened to have me removed as Chief Justice over my obsession with my birth mother Gerd's escape from custody in Standora. Their discovery of the grimoire should have cemented my fate.

I licked my lips before I asked, "Why is everyone covering for me?"

"Talbert informed us of the suspected spy within the Balance home Temple." Mya sighed. "As much as I dislike politics and lies, someone helped Gerd escape and someone made sure that damn grimoire ended up back in your hands. You were set up. You didn't choose to join the renegades. For now, we simply can't trust anyone outside of the city."

"What about Duke Marco and Magistrate DiCook?"

Again, Mya sighed. "They fear we have done something to you. I think it best if you are the one to tell them what happened."

For all of my righteous indignation over doing the right thing, I didn't know how I was going to face my equals, much less my staff. Nor was I sure I trusted myself.

Or that I ever would again.

Chapter 2

The visit with Ming Wei went well enough High Sister Mya moved me to one of the second floor treatment rooms. I was shocked by the changes in Yanaba's squire. Ming Wei no longer tried to comb her hair over the left side of her head to cover her scars. Nor did she have the painfully shy bearing from before.

No, this new version stood straight and proud. I was happy for her even if I was ashamed of the circumstances that brought about this change. While she still flinched if a man moved too suddenly around her, she wasn't running away as she had when she first came to Balance.

A fortnight later, Mya released me from Child though she said we would continue our private meetings once a week. Since she was already coming to Balance to treat and train Ming Wei, she planned to talk to me after they were finished.

Chief Warden Little Bear and Warden Gina accompanied Ming Wei to escort me back to Balance. They both wore wide grins, and Gina carried one of my uniforms and my weapons.

"We can't let you go out in public looking like a sailor coming off a three-day bender," she commented.

"Thank you," I said. "Are you also planning to braid my hair?"

"Of course," she proclaimed. "What did I just say about looking a sailor off a three-day bender?"

Once I was properly dressed and my hair braided and pinned up, I buckled on my sword and stowed my knives in their various sheaths. For the first time in two months, I didn't feel totally naked.

Gina, Ming Wei and I returned to the first floor where Little Bear was speaking quietly with High Sister Mya. The priestess broke into smiles and hugged me.

"If you need anything, Anthea—" she started.

"I have a feeling you'll know before I do." I gave her a wry smile, and she laughed.

When we stepped outside of the Temple of Child, cool air caressed my face. The terrible heat of the summer was gone. I nodded to the warden on main door duty. She nodded back. There was no change in her body temperature. I was simply another person who passed through their doors. As Mya had said, my reservations were mine, not anyone else's.

While my party and I walked down the main boulevard of the Temple District, the muttering from passersby started. There was no sense taking a back alley to Balance. The citizens were going to gossip regardless. It didn't mean I had to like it though.

When we strode up the steps of Balance, Warden Ailyn stood guard at the main doors. She broke out into a huge grin. "Welcome home, Chief Justice."

I noticed both set of doors were open. The statue of Balance Herself stared at me from her dais in the courtroom. I turned to Little Bear. "Why isn't court being conducted this morning?"

"Justice Yanaba canceled it in lieu of a more important event." He nodded toward the courtroom. "They were waiting on you to begin."

Curious and more than a little concerned about Yanaba arbitrarily closing the court, I strode into the main courtroom.

And nearly jumped out of my skin when a throng of people yelled, "Welcome home, Chief Justice."

It wasn't just the folks from Balance. I quickly counted the different badges. Members from all twelve Temples were here, along with people from the Healers Guild, Orrin's peacekeepers, and Duke Marco and his family. Rounding out the group were personnel from the Jing embassy, including Ambassador Quan himself.

My own squire Nathan ran up to me. I half-expected a hug. Instead, he executed a perfect bow. "May I escort you to your seat, Lady Justice?"

"Why, thank you, Squire Nathan."

He moved to my left side and extended his right elbow. With any other justice, he would have wrapped the fingers of my left hand around the crook of his arm. But I could see, so he adjusted appropriately.

I took his arm. Waves of pride crashed into my psyche. So I took a little chance.

Nathan?

He quivered at the touch of my mind to his, but he kept his solemn pace. *Yes, m'lady?*

I apologize for my behavior in the garden. No assigning blame to others. No excuses to justify my behavior. No waiting to make amends when we were alone. But I still felt the need to keep this between the two of us.

I accept your apology, m'lady. Warmth flooded from him physically and emotionally. Maybe I hadn't ruined my relationship with him after all.

We reached the chair at the head of the table my staff had set up in the courtroom, but I didn't take the seat. One-by-one my staff came to me with their good wishes. And I threw protocol out the window and hugged them all.

The celebration died down shortly after Second Afternoon since everyone had their own duties to attend. However, I noticed Luc, Claudia, and Talbert lingering behind. I leaned over to Elizabeth seated on my right and whispered, "Is there a private conversation we need to have with the remaining clergy?"

"You need to have," she corrected. "Though Yanaba and I would like to be included." She hesitated a moment before she added, "Can we please have no more secrets between us?"

I sighed. "All right. Squires?"

Nathan and Ming Wei ran up to my chair. "Would you escort the justices to our reception room?" I turned to Luc. "High Brother, would you and Sister Claudia please stay for a short discussion?"

At their nods, I looked at Talbert. "Would you please assist me in take a few bottles of wine into the Balance reception room?"

He grinned, the first time I ever recalled him wearing anything but a slight smile, and grabbed as many bottles from the table in the courtroom as he could safely carry.

"Chief Warden?"

Little Bear snapped to attention. "Would you assist Sivan in bringing us some fresh goblets? And then join us. I need wise counsel from both of you."

His face shifted from orange to red. "Yes, m'lady."

I climbed to my feet. Despite it being mid-afternoon, lethargy dragged on my very bones. So I was extremely careful not to try to carry more bottles than I could handle. It would be damn near sacrilege to Vintner to waste good Pana wine.

Once we were settled in the reception room, and the other seats kicked their wardens out to Gina's great amusement though she wasn't included either, I stood and circled the room, casting my wards. This meeting needed to be private on more levels than I could count.

When I reached my chair, I remained standing. "First, I need to make amends. High Brother Luc, Sister Claudia, I sincerely apologize. My jealousy over the two of you doing your duty has no place in our world. I never wanted to see anything happen to your son."

I swallowed the lump of shame at the back of my throat. "Chief Justice Elizabeth, Justice Yanaba, you tried to warn me of the path I was taking, and I didn't listen. I apologize for allowing my arrogance to get in the way of all of our duties.

"And to all of you, thank you for believing I could possibly be redeemed. I pray to the Twelve I can live up to your regard." I grabbed the arms of my chair and shakily sat down.

"You were set up, Anthea." Talbert poured wine for Elizabeth and himself before he passed the bottle to Claudia. "The renegades manipulated both Gerd and you."

When Luc started to protest, Talbert held up his hands. "I'm not saying Gerd is totally innocent by any means." He lowered his hands. "My concern is what is happening in Standora." He looked at me. "I've already shared my concerns with Elizabeth and Yanaba."

"Reverend Mother Alara," I murmured. Her siding with the renegades was the only way her recent actions made sense unless she was going senile like my predecessor Chief Justice Penelope had.

"I have to agree with him." Yanaba's disgust and frustration beat against my mind. "She made a point of having me present at the alleged destruction of that blasted grimoire. And yet, Gerd brought the same damn tome into Orrin."

"We cannot voice these things outside of this room or a convocation," Elizabeth said.

"Unfortunately, I've had plenty of time to think about what happened." I took a sip of wine. After two months of only water, I truly appreciated the small things at my own Temple. "The demons are using the renegades to study us. Learn how to manipulate us. After nearly a thousand years, they haven't been able to defeat us in straight battles, though the Twelve know it has been close at times. So the demons are taking the lessons they've learned from the Assassins Guild about how humans work mentally and emotionally and applying them to us."

Talbert nodded. "That is my Reverend Father's assessment as well. However, I believe we've cleaned out any problems within the Orrin Temples."

"What do you mean?" I asked.

"Remember how we were truthspelling each other in Tandor prior to the siege," Luc said.

I nodded. "I take it you did the same here in Orrin."

"Everyone from the clergy to the cooks." Claudia glanced at the others before she added, "Love did the same thing after you arrested Gerd."

"Balance help me," I murmured. "Things seemed so simple last winter."

"We've been truthspelling the duke's employees and everyone at Government House," Luc said. "But we're doing it on Duke Marco and Magistrate DiCook's authority."

"Several of the guilds have asked for us to interrogate their members about their allegiance as well," Yanaba added. "But there's nothing legally we can do about the general populace or the uncooperative guilds."

"There's only one problem with your interrogations." I leaned my right elbow on the table and rested my chin on my fist. "There may be a sub personality inside a person's mind they don't know about."

"Like the one created for High Brother Aduba to infiltrate the renegades in Tandor?" Luc said.

"Yes." I sighed. "I'm wondering if they didn't do something similar to Peacekeeper Dante or Barbora the seamstress." I looked at Talbert. "Any suggestions, High Brother?"

"I think we've done everything we can for now." He tapped the side of his goblet. Something else bothered him, but I had too much to catch up on to worry about his unknown statement yet.

I turned to Sivan. "Where are Cat and Dog? The only thing Mya would tell me is that they were recovering." More guilt tore at me. The two street children had been my eyes and ears until Gerd took control of their minds.

"Govind and his wife have taken them in," Sivan said. "One good thing out of all this mess is that the street children are starting to trust the Temple of Mother again. It's slow progress, and they refuse to talk to the three priestesses remaining from Bianca's rule—"

"The fact Leocadia's making any progress is good news." I lifted my goblet in the direction of the Temple of Mother and took another sip.

"I also owe much to you and Little Bear," I continued. "First, you had to deal with the chaos of having a senile chief justice, and then the chaos of a demon-mad chief justice." Little Bear opened his mouth, but I waved my right hand. "No, you two kept this Temple going. Yanaba will have her hands full with her babe soon, and Elizabeth will be transferring to the new Duchy of Anacapa. Unfortunately, that means you've dealt with the Reverend Mother more than I have. I want your suggestions on how best we move forward."

"Very carefully?" Little Bear added a wry smile. The rest of the assembly laughed except for Sivan.

"You do realize we are talking treason here, Chief Justice?" she said.

"I know." I shrugged. "In for a copper, in for a crown. I just wish I knew how to broach the issue with the queen that didn't find all our heads at the wrong end of a sword."

"There's one additional matter you should be aware of." Talbert rubbed his chin, which was never a good sign. "The crown princess has requested to be informed of your recovery through my Reverend Father."

I straightened. "Why?"

"The Duke of Standora wishes to speak with you in person and privately." Talbert shrugged. "Forgive me, Anthea, but that was all I was told. I sent the message yesterday when Mya informed us she believed you were ready to resume your seat."

I sat back in my chair. Balance take me. What could Crown Princess Chiara or her husband possibly want with me?

Unless the Reverend Mother had decided to take a more direct approach to get me out of the way.

Chapter 3

◈

Four days later, the smell of Jing tea mixed with the dusty odor of old tomes in my office in the Temple of Balance. I stared at White Eagle, the Duke of Standora and Lord General of the Queen's Army, who sat in a visitor chair on the other side of my desk.

Luc did the same from his seat next to White Eagle.

"Are you jesting with us, Your Grace?" I blurted.

"Do I look like I am joking, Chief Justice?" he said before scowling at me. He held up one of the folded and sealed letters he'd dumped on my desk. "You are to take these to the Matriarch of the Diné as a representative of Queen Teodora of Issura."

"B-but neither I nor High Brother Luc are in any shape to travel to Diné, much less lead a diplomatic delegation." I squeezed my cup, wishing the warmth of the ceramic would heat the bones of my hands. Ever since Ming Wei pulled me from the brink of succumbing to the demon grimoire, I felt constantly chilled. Not even sitting in the Temple kitchen while our cook Deborah baked could heat my body, much less my spirit.

"The Matriarch of the Diné requested you two specifically in lieu of myself or the crown princess." A twitch of White Eagle's lips wouldn't qualify as a smile on anyone else, but it was the closest the duke had come to expressing any emotion in my presence. "Apparently, you two made an impression on their Reverend Father of Conflict, and the Diné refuse to speak with anyone else from Issura."

I cleared my throat. It would be best to get things out in the open now, no matter how annoyed the duke may become with me.

"Are you aware the Reverend Father happens to be my biological sire, Your Grace?"

"Better him than me." The duke waggled his eyebrows. A full-fledged grin filled his face.

I stared at him. "This isn't funny."

"Your Grace, with all due respect," Luc said firmly. "There are higher ranked members of the Temples who would be better equipped for such an important assignment."

"You're also the highest rank Temple clergy who have their own houses in order," the duke snapped.

"There's been quite a bit of trauma between the two of us—" Luc tried again.

"High Sister Mya has assured the other seats of Orrin the chief justice is mentally stable enough to resume her duties." White Eagle's eyes narrowed. "And I've heard your fighting abilities with your crutches exceed your skill with a sword when you are not indulging in Vintner's gifts. Is there something else you're hiding besides your personal intimate relations that would inhibit either of your diplomatic skills?"

Air froze in my chest. If he accused us of relations prior to the breeding edict issued last spring, Luc and I could lose our heads.

"It sounds like Your Grace is aware of our multitude of sins," Luc said dryly.

Balance help me, there was one last sin. But if I admitted to the possession of the damn grimoire, every seat of Orrin and every member of my staff faced losing their heads in their conspiracy to free me from the demons' influence. Or maybe that's what our enemies were hoping for.

"We're both concerned about the priestesses with child under our roofs, Your Grace," I murmured. "Especially after Gerd killed the babe Sister Claudia of Love carried."

The duke's nostrils flared. "You killed Gerd in defense of your fellow clergy, did you not?"

"Yes, Your Grace." Balance, I wanted to shake some sense into him.

"She's dead. The remaining priestesses with child are safe. You are going to Diné, Chief Justice, High Brother Luc will accompany you, and you will deliver the queen's letters to their Matriarch. That is a command from your orders' leaders and your queen." The duke saluted me with his cup. "End of discussion."

"Reverend Mother Alara agreed to me leaving Orrin?" I said.

White Eagle looked at Luc. "She truly does not understand what 'end of discussion' means, does she?"

"Only when she says it, Your Grace."

I could handle the jibes, but I clenched my fists on my lap. Terrible fear hit me about the Reverend Mother's motives, and again, if I said the wrong thing, more people than me would lose their heads.

"Forgive my bad manners, Your Grace," I murmured.

A hint of sympathy crossed his features. "Anthea, if I was forced to kill my mother, I would need the care of Child, too. There's no shame in admitting you needed their help, anymore than if you needed to see a healer for a physical injury. I know you're upset by the incident, but you need to move on. And you know Thief will let us know if you two fail to go."

For the briefest of moments, I almost told him of our suspicions concerning my own Reverend Mother. The duke had been a Conflict priest himself before he'd received a special dispensation to marry Crown Princess Chiara. But what if the Reverend Mother had twisted his perceptions? Or those of the queen or the crown princess?

Instead, I swallowed my accusations and said, "Yes, Your Grace."

"However, you two handled the siege admirably and managed to evacuate most of the populace . . ." While he spoke, the duke reached for a scrap piece of parchment. Using the ink and quill my clerks left on my desk, he scribbled something, sanded it dry, and handed the note to Luc.

Luc's eyes widened as he read. He looked at me. *The queen doesn't trust the heads of our Temples. She fears it's more complicated than a few spies within.*

The duke didn't ask me to ward my office because doing so would alert his escort that secrets were being shared. I turned to him and nodded once.

". . . both the queen and your superiors trust you to accomplish these negotiations." The duke pushed to his feet, and Luc and I automatically rose.

"We will not fail the queen, Your Grace," I said. "Thank you for your trust."

White Eagle held up his right hand. "No need to escort me out, Chief Justice, High Brother. I must pay a visit to Duke Marco. Good morningtide to you both."

Once he left my office, Luc and I stared at each other. It was the first time we'd been alone together since my mother had killed his son. The weight of this new task sat on the silence between us.

Luc lowered himself back to his chair and took a sip of tea.

I wasn't sure what to do. I expected him to leave on the duke's heels. So I resumed my seat as well. We definitely couldn't discuss the duke's note. At my pointed look at Luc's hand, he stuffed the scrap in the duke's empty cup and concentrated. Wisps of smoke floated from the ceramic as the parchment smoldered.

Unfortunately, that meant we were back to staring at each other.

"I don't know—" I started to say at the same moment he said, "I know you hate me—"

We both stopped and stared at each other again.

"I never hated you," I murmured. "And you have every right to be angry with me—"

"I knew exactly what Gerd was capable of." He exhaled and ran his fingers through his hair. His curls fell past his chin, far longer than he normally kept it, but his face was clean shaven, and he smelled like he'd bathed recently. "So did Claudia for that matter. You're right. They are using our own idiocy against us."

He looked at me. "If anything, I owe you an apology."

"Me?"

"I bedded you because I knew you couldn't conceive. It was . . . safe." His skin turn crimson.

"You know you were assigned to me in the hope you would seduce me, don't you?" I said.

"Wait. What?" He cocked his head.

"It was part of manipulating me." I shook my head. "Give me someone to care about." I waved my right hand. "And then, the edict—"

"Its purpose was to drive a wedge between us." Disgust dripped from his voice.

"Not totally. We do need children with Light and Balance talents." I drummed my fingertips against the grain of my desktop. "It's like I said the other day, and you did just now. Demons don't feel emotions the same way we do. It has taken them nearly ten centuries to learn how we interact and function together."

"So what do we do now?" he asked.

"Start preparing for the journey to Diné—" I said.

Luc chuckled. "No, I meant between you and me. Our personal relationship."

Balance, help me, I didn't want to lose him. But I had so much in my mind and spirit I needed to sort out. My feelings thundered over my training in logic.

"Can we start over?" I asked. "Maybe not share a bed until we return from this diplomatic trip?"

He nodded slowly. "If that's what you wish." But from his tone, it wasn't what he wanted.

"Luc, I'm scared." My limbs trembled, and I hugged myself. "I came so close to being swallowed by the grimoire. Just like Gerd was. A-and I was about to strike Nathan. Possibly even kill him. I would have if Ming Wei hadn't stopped me. I worry Mya is wrong, and I'm still under demon influence. I fear I'll hurt or kill you when we're out in the middle of the desert with no one else to keep me in check."

He held out his right hand. After a moment, I unwrapped my arms and clasped his fingers with my left.

"You won't do anything to harm me. Do you know why?"

I shook my head.

"Because you are stronger than they know. And despite anyone's machinations, I love you, and you love me." He squeezed my hand. "If that's not enough, remember all the people who welcomed you home the other day. They all care about you, too."

I returned the squeeze. "The same goes for you. Or is DiCook still banned from your Temple?"

"If you're mocking me, then you have definitely recovered." But Luc lifted my hand and kissed the back. A flutter of desire ran through me despite my suggestion to start over with our relationship.

"If you miss my taunting, then thank you very much for bathing," I responded.

He rose from his chair and grabbed his crutches. "And thank you for not stabbing me or beheading me."

We both grinned, and he gave a slight bow before leaving my office.

Once Luc left, Warden Long Feather peered around the edge of the doorjamb. "Do you wish you door closed, m'lady?"

"Leave it open for now, Warden."

"As you wish." He hesitated a moment.

"Is there something on your mind?" I asked. Long Feather wasn't one to poke about the bush, but then he usually followed the chain of command. It left me a little curious about whatever subject he didn't want to discuss with Little Bear.

"May I have your permission to speak freely and privately, Chief Justice?"

I nodded. He stepped into my office and closed the door behind him.

"I would like permission to accompany you on your diplomatic mission to Diné."

I gestured for him to take a seat before I folded my hands on top of my desk. "Before you continue, have you considered that a great number of people who accompany me outside the walls of Orrin end up dead?"

"I am aware of the risks, m'lady."

"Also, considering that the Duke of Standora literally just handed me the orders—" I held up the scroll he had delivered on behalf of the queen. "—I have to assume you were eavesdropping."

"The High Brother of Thief has had his clergy and wardens training the rest of us in their techniques." Long Feather's skin remained its normal yellowish orange. "He pointed out we've been trying to catch up to the renegades. We need to get ahead."

Apparently, Talbert and his people had been working hard for the two months I spent at Child. "What is your logic for joining this expedition?"

"Warden Gina has been teaching us the Diné language," Long Feather said. "Given her proficiency, you will take her with you on your diplomatic mission in lieu of Chief Warden Little Bear. Also, it's no secret Chief Justice Elizabeth has requested Gina's services as her new chief warden. Given the crown's trust in you as their representative, you will need someone fluent in Diné when she leaves. This mission will allow me to practice my language skills."

"And eavesdrop some more?" I teased.

He smiled. "Only to protect you and the interests of the queen, m'lady."

"If you're sure you want this assignment?"

"I'm sure, m'lady." The trill of his excitement tickled my psyche. It was so very odd to feel others' emotions again. But Mya said she needed the shackles to keep everyone's feelings from intruding in order for me to understand and deal with my own emotions. She didn't want the demons to get to me again.

"All right. You may accompany me to Diné," I said.

Long Feather leapt to his feet. "Thank you, m'lady."

I chuckled. "Before you dance in celebration, please have Nathan fetch me a hot pot of tea."

"Yes, m'lady." He bowed and left my office.

I couldn't fault the young man's confidence and enthusiasm. But my guilt crawled out of its hole and whispered I'd just condemned Long Feather to a very short life span.

Chapter 4

A week later, all arrangements had been completed. Yanaba and Elizabeth had already requested a second contingent of Balance wardens while I was being treated by Child. Little Bear would be kept occupied kicking them into shape while I was gone. Elizabeth would take eleven of them with her once the construction of the Temple of Balance on the isle of Tuqan was completed. One of the new trainees would replace Gina here in Orrin.

Little Bear and I sat in my office, reviewing assignments for the trip.

"I'm sending Dezba and Mylon to accompany you in addition to Gina and Long Feather." He gave me a look like he expected a battle from me.

I merely asked, "Why?"

"Dezba knows the language, and Mylon won't have to work as hard to stay awake all night during the journey across the desert," Little Bear quipped.

I stared at my chief warden.

"You also need an escort befitting your station as both a chief justice and the queen's ambassador."

When I raised my right eyebrow, he added, "Also, they can watch each other's backs as well as yours. And before you start complaining, Chief Warden Nicholas is taking the same number to guard the high brother."

I folded my arms over my chest. "I know you, Little Bear. What's really running through your mind?"

A deadly mien slid over his face. "We have no idea how many demons or skinwalkers are lurking in the desert between here and Diné," he said softly. "The Temple survivors from Tandor were picked off one by one when they sought help last spring."

I shouldn't have needed the reminder. My nightmares about Gerd killing Claudia and Luc's babe were divided by nightmares from when Luc and I were sent to Tandor and the demon siege of the city.

"Is that the real reason Han and Jax are sending their seconds?" I muttered.

"Talbert is volunteering two of his people as well," Little Bear said.

I leaned my elbows on my desk surface. "That isn't going to look good to the Diné Matriarch and her council. It signals we don't trust them."

"I really doubt that's how she will take it." Little Bear made a slashing motion with his hand. "Not after the reports of the siege from their own Temple personnel—"

Someone pounded on my closed office door. My staff wouldn't interrupt Little Bear and me unless it was urgent.

"Enter!"

Nathan opened the door and bowed. "Sisters Claudia and Zihna of Love are here to speak with you, Lady Justice, along with two of their wardens." The boy seemed determined to be the perfect squire since I returned to my Temple. I needed to send a message to High Sister Mya about his extreme behavior. Balance knew what emotional damage I'd inflicted in my arrogance, and She knew I didn't have a moment to make a formal visit with the seat of Child.

I glanced at Little Bear. He shook his head. So, he didn't know what was going on either. However, I didn't get a sense of alarm from anyone standing outside my office.

"Very well, but their wardens are going to have to listen in through the door same as my wardens." My teasing had its effect. Little Bear's skin heated after my discussion of Long Feather's eavesdropping. However, I could hear Warden Ailyn titter in the corridor.

The bells on the sisters' robes jingled as they entered my office. Both women wore their public veils, but Claudia was a handspan taller than Zihna. It was tight in my office with just one visitor. Four adults and a child made the space claustrophobic. I hadn't been joking about the wardens listening in to our conversation because they simply couldn't fit in my office.

Claudia inclined her head. "Thank you for hearing us on such short notice."

"Let me guess. You wish to join my little expedition to Diné?"

Humor flowed from both women. Claudia handed me a scroll. "High Sister Dragonfly gives her permission for us to accompany you."

I accepted the scroll, but I didn't bother cracking the seal. Whatever my personal feelings about the woman, she wasn't the type for subterfuge.

"Sisters, this is not a clamming trip to Sandy Spit," I said.

"We're aware," Claudia said dryly. "However, we also have heard the stories from our sisters who took part in the Battle of Tandor. Our purpose in accompanying you is twofold. You'll need every talent you can manage if you encounter demons or skinwalkers." She sucked in a harsh breath. "And we need to replace the child I lost."

I frowned, but I didn't have to ask why Dragonfly didn't trust sending one of her priestesses to another Temple of Light within Issura. Nor did I have to ask why the high sister didn't press our remaining brothers of Light.

"Sister Zihna, are you sure this is the course of action you wish to take?" I asked. "The trip across the desert will not be an easy one, and I cannot guarantee your safety."

"She even questioned the sanity of her own wardens who volunteered to accompany her," Little Bear added.

The sisters laughed while I scowled at my chief warden.

"Well, you did," he said in an accusing voice.

"Are you two coming with us as well?" I asked of the Love wardens standing just outside my door.

"Yes, m'lady," they both replied.

"I know you, Warden Jocasta," I hinted. "And your associate is?"

Jocasta gestured at her companion. "This is Warden Ekta."

"Ekta? Isn't that an Apache name?" I asked.

"Yes, m'lady." The warden bobbed her head. "According to my family's stories, my ancestor Ekta was a survivor of the massacre. A babe hidden by her mother's corpse from the demons. The name has been passed down."

I didn't have to ask what massacre. Every child in Issura knew the story of how the entire Apache Empire stalled a demon army long enough for reinforcements from the surrounding nations to arrive. The names of the survivors were included in a Conflict prayer through out the Long Continents.

"Well met, Warden." I smiled. "Please do your best to stay away from the Balance wardens. I don't want your high sister to complain you've picked up their bad habits."

Ekta's mouth dropped open at my rude statement. However, Jocasta leaned closer to Ekta and said, "They only reflect the manners of their seat."

"Really, Warden Jocasta?" At Ekta's appalled expression, Little Bear sniffed. "We are quite mad in our own right without any of our resident justices's help."

We all roared with laughter. Even young Nathan giggled.

"All right," I said when I could catch my breath. "Ladies of Love, we're leaving right after morning services at the Temple of Light."

"We will be ready, Lady Justice," Claudia said. Both priestesses bowed.

"Wardens, make sure you and your charges bring extra water skins," Little Bear called out.

"We will," Jocasta assured him before she followed the sisters.

Ekta's expression said she believed we all should be treated by Child.

I nodded to Nathan, and he closed my office door behind him.

"Are you going to be all right with Claudia accompanying you?" Little Bear said softly.

"I need to be, my friend," I said. "For all of our sakes."

Chapter 5

We gathered in front of Light shortly before First Morning. Any hope I had of keeping this diplomatic party small flew south with the migrating birds. Duke Marco insisted on sending his sister Lady Alessa to advise me in the subject of trade, which meant she brought a handmaid and two guards. Magistrate DiCook insisted that four peacekeepers escort us to augment the wardens. At least, he put Leyti, who I knew could keep his head in a crisis, in charge of them.

High Mother Leocadia couldn't leave because she was still dealing with the aftermath of her predecessor's crimes. However, she insisted her personal chef Ademaro, the one she brought with her when she was assigned to Orrin, accompany us.

Add in to the mix two clergy and two wardens each from the Love, Conflict, Thief, and Wildling Temples. To top everything off, High Brother Ben waited until late last night before he told me he was volunteering himself and one of his priestesses to our party. Which meant two more wardens as well. Ben's excuse was that he owed Luc and me for breaking the mind control spell Gerd had cast upon him.

In an effort to find some peace in the midst of the pandemonium, I entered the Temple of Light. Gina followed me inside, and she surprised me by sitting beside me on the bench. A few citizens looked at us curiously, but otherwise, they withdrew into their own thoughts.

The clergy of Light entered the sanctuary, their voices raised in song. Sister Shi Hua's soprano elevated the morning prayer-song to a new level of harmony. The loveliness made me wonder what the dawn services in Jing sounded like with the blend of voices.

Luc had no problem using his crutches to kneel before the statue of Light and the eternal flame that burned at His base. However, Brothers Jeremy and Garbhan assisted Shi Hua to her knees. The young woman had entered her final trimester of her pregnancy, and I swore each day her middle was a handspan larger that the day before.

Unlike Balance's severity, Light's image welcomed anyone and everyone. He reminded me of my maternal grandfather Kam. Not in appearance so much, but His carved smile matched Kam's good humor. I missed him, and I often wondered if this last year would have turned out differently if he hadn't taken a poisoned knife met for me.

The service turned to call and response. Mine and Gina's voices joined the other worshippers' in Light's warm embrace. Even when Death takes us we would still see Him one last time.

The Reverend Mother may have been playing games with my emotions by telling me there was a prophesy about me and by setting me up to bond with the Light priest assigned to my circuit. However, Luc was everything to me Light promised. Joy. Illumination. Truth.

And most of all love.

However, Balance and Light didn't have so much tragedy weighting Them when They first came into existence. Did I really think I was better than the Twelve Themselves? That I could overcome all the problems set in my path.

Yes, we *can.*

An open hand was in front of me. I looked up at Luc. Then I looked around the sanctuary. Most of the civilians had left. The few who remained were asking for personal blessings from the other Light clergy.

I released the air caught in my lungs, but I couldn't speak, out loud or silently. Taking Luc's hand, I stood, squeezed his fingers and released them. Together, we left the Temple of Light.

And for some strange reason, my nerves danced under my skin the same way they did the night we sailed out of the harbor for Tandor late last winter. I didn't bother praying for guidance from Balance. The one time she spoke to me, she told me to jump off a cliff.

As we traveled south on the National Road, I could see the damage to the cobblestones and surrounding vegetation from the passing of the queen's army on its way to our rescue. Normally, the duke would have repaired the road, but there was no reason to waste the money and effort.

No merchants traveled along this section anymore. Not with the loss of Tandor in Issura and Rambla in Cant. There was simply no place for the merchant caravans to restock their personal water supplies even if they used camels as their beasts of burden.

I patted Nassa's neck as she plodded along the road. The oases through the Valley of the Lost were well marked. We should be fine. I didn't know what I was worrying about.

"May I ask what you're fretting about?" Claudia said. She and Sister Migina of Conflict flanked me while we rode. Claudia had removed her veil now that we were several leagues from the city walls, probably to enjoy the warmth of the sun on her skin.

"Everything," I answered. "I can't stop worrying about everything."

"What specifically?" Migina asked.

I eyed first Claudia, then Migina. "You two sound suspiciously like High Sister Mya."

"With all due respect, Chief Justice, do you really believe you're the only one who has ever sought Child's help?" Migina shook her head.

"Everyone in Orrin knowing my personal business is one of the reasons I was on the edge of madness," I complained.

"It's not like the citizens are watching your every bowel movement," Migina said.

"No, that's the wardens," Claudia teased. The two priestesses roared with laughter.

"To answer your original question, Sister Claudia, and to change the Twelve-forsaken subject," I said. "I was thinking about the lack of repairs on the National Road."

"It is troubling," Claudia murmured. "However, Duke Marco wasn't expecting to support the queen's troops and an entire city's worth of refugees this year."

"Unfortunately, the losses of Tandor and Rambla also leave a huge gap in Issura and Cant's defenses." Migina pursed her lips. "Restoring the settlements on the Anacapa Islands won't be enough if another cache of demon eggs are brought to our shores."

"You fear demons may have more eggs somewhere?" I asked.

A wry smile tilted the Conflict priestess's mouth. "Of course they did, but I'm more worried about what may be lurking in the Valley of the Lost. I read the reports from my order who were with you in Tandor."

"Where would we put a new fortress?" I asked.

"I don't know if it would have to be a fortress," she said. "There just needs to be fresh water facilities."

"But where would we dig wells?" Claudia asked. "That close to the coast, any well is likely to be contaminated with sea water."

"A good portion of Tandor's aqueduct is still intact," I mused. "We can check it as we head east."

My statement launched a conversation of possible ways to capture the water from the mountains that was probably pouring onto the sands of the desert for the last six months.

Rather than making camp for the night, we continued at an easy pace. We would stop at the last watering hole before the National Road curved out into the desert and spend the day there. Traveling through the Valley of the Lost during the sunlight hours, even in the autumn, was not wise.

With the moonless night, Claudia, the Wildlings, and I took point. I linked with Sisquoc and Farrah as they scouted ahead. I didn't need conventional light to see, so I called out holes and uneven stones for the mounted members of our party. Claudia and her steed matched mine and Nassa's pace.

The sister of Love seemed determined to keep an eye on me. Part of me wondered why. The other part didn't want to know. However, my curiosity won out.

"Sister, why are you trying so hard to be kind to me?" I asked softly.

She exhaled. The green cloud of her breath dissipated rapidly in the dryer air. "I'm not sure that is a subject we should be discussing during this diplomatic mission." She glanced behind her. "Nor should we be discussing this subject with other ears around."

What about silent speech? I asked.

Claudia's laughter jingled in my mind like the silver bells on her robes. *All right. The issue is I admire you. You swooped in as if you were Balance Herself and rescued us in Love from a horrible situation.*

Her esteem teased its way through my guilt and jealousy. I didn't know how to respond to that.

All of us assumed Gerd lied about you and Luc. She sighed, and this time, the guilt I felt wasn't mine. *I was honored to conceive a child with a brother of Light, but I swear to Love neither the high sister nor I would intentionally hurt you.*

I know. I tried to swallow my own anguish. *You tried to tell me that more than once. It was never you I was angry with. It was Gerd. She hated her birth parents so much she literally let it destroy her. And she didn't care who else she harmed along the way.*

Nassa whinnied at the pressure of my knees against her ribs. I forced my thighs to relax and patted her neck.

High Sister Mya made me realize I was following Gerd's path. I resented her so much for taking my sight, and then my ability to have children. I let that resentment spilled over in my regard for you. I swear to Balance I never wanted to see harm come to yours and Luc's son. And I most definitely never wanted you to suffer my fate.

So how do we go forward from here if none of the issues between us was our fault? Claudia asked.

Mya is right about one thing, I said. *It's going to take time for all of us to heal from the destruction Gerd wrought over the last couple of years.*

True, but I'd still like to be friends.

I'll work on it, I said. *I've never had anyone want to be my friend before. Can you be patient with me?*

Always.

Chapter 6

Late the next afternoon after we woke, I performed some easy stretching exercises with the other priestesses. Whatever calluses I had from ten years on circuit seemed to have disappeared.

"Chief Justice, you know with the current edict, you have an excuse for being in the saddle every night like the Love sisters," Migina quipped.

"You're one to talk," Zihna shot back. "The chief justice has more offers to ride than you do."

The other women laughed at the young priestesses' ribald patter.

It was odd. I never had this type of easy camaraderie with my classmates at the home Temple of Balance. Like I told Claudia the night before, I never had anyone who wanted to be friends with me. My eyes scared nearly everyone I met. As for the other novices at Balance, they couldn't see my eyes, but they avoided me since I was considered a troublemaker.

It didn't take long to break down our camp. Nassa and the other horses seemed to know they wouldn't get much to drink for the next two days. They took long draughts from the water hole.

As the sun dipped below the western horizon, we set out on the National Road once again. By full dark, someone was snoring behind me. I turned to look. Warden Long Feather and Peacekeeper Jaime had the last watch of the day. It was definitely one of them from the way their heads drooped. Or maybe they were snoring in unison from the volume of sound. I wasn't sure how they managed to sleep in the saddle. It was a talent I'd never acquired in all my years on circuit.

"What is it with men and snoring?" Migina complained.

"That's one of the wonderful things about Love." Claudia chuckled. "Once we've completed worship, they leave."

"Don't you miss holding someone afterward?" Migina asked.

"There's a difference between cuddling and sex," Zihna called over her shoulder.

I could feel Sister Farrah listening to the conversation through me.

Riding alongside Zihna, Sister Nina of Vintner laughed. It was the first time I noticed our delegation had split up between female and male clergy as we rode tonight.

"Do you think a person's need for cuddling comes from not having enough in their everyday lives?" I asked.

"That sounds more like a question for Child," Nina said.

Claudia pursed her lips. "I take it the priestesses in your home Temple aren't big on hugs for the child novices."

I burst out laughing. "Any touching for us are from wardens guiding us from place to place or the assistants helping us with our daily grooming. If the ordained justices touch us, it's usually punishment."

Sympathy and outrage flowed from the other priestesses, including Farrah who was scouting ahead of us.

That's awful, the Wildling priestess said.

"Touch is how we at Balance understand the world." I shrugged. "It can be a blessing and a curse."

"Well, if I were assigned to Balance," Migina said. "I sure as Conflict would be taking advantage of the edict and experiencing as much good touching as I could possibly get."

I looked at her. "How did you not get assigned to Love?"

"She's only interested in her own pleasure," Zihna teased. "Not anyone else's."

"I didn't hear you complain during the Vintner's Festival," Migina returned.

"That's because my mouth was full," Zihna retorted.

Even I had to laugh at the younger priestesses' antics.

Migina decided to ignore Zihna. "In all seriousness, Chief Justice, all the men at Conflict would be interested in entertaining you."

Claudia made a low sound in her throat.

"What?" Migina waved her free hand nonchalantly. "She needs some recommendations." The sister leaned closer to me. "I would suggest Brother Yas we when return to Orrin. His name may mean 'snow' in Diné, but in bed, he's anything but."

My hands turned red, and I was sure my face was the same color. Only the other women's lack of night vision prevented them from seeing my mortification.

"Migina," Claudia growled.

"Oh, I'm sorry." The Conflict priestess actually sounded contrite. "I didn't know the two of you—"

"Stop!" Realizing she had shouted, Claudia lowered her voice. "For the love of the Twelve, please stop. We have another twelve days through the desert, and if I have to hear you extoll and rank the bed play of every adult in Orrin, I swear I will leave your body for the coyotes."

"I, uh, well . . ." Migina lost her talkativeness.

"Sister Migina, I know you are trying to help," I murmured. "And I appreciate your honesty and enthusiasm, but we all need to maintain some decorum while we are guests in Diné."

She cleared her throat. "I apologize for overstepping, Chief Justice."

"And don't attack any Diné for intercourse," I added. "Go to their Temple of Love to relieve any . . . itches."

"Unless you are actually itching down there, then please go see a healer," Zihna said.

The priestesses and wardens around us roared with laughter.

Maybe I had found my true sisters in Orrin after all.

Chapter 7

The heat of the desert made it difficult to sleep the first few days after we left Issura despite the shelters and caves along the route. We were reliving the sweltering summer. I noticed several of our party wrapped scarves, veils, or sections of their robes over their eyes to simulate the night in order to help them sleep. To me, the sun was a bloody orb floating through a dark blue sky, the same as the moon. Its brightness did not bother me.

Since I was waking early, I repeatedly offered to take one of the afternoon watches, but the wardens and peacekeepers refused. I joined them anyway because I couldn't sleep. The heat of the ground seemed to seep under the shade of my tent.

I definitely owed Leocadia for allowing her chef Ademaro to travel with us. Sisquoc, Farrah, and their wardens would hunt for us. Ademaro would then roast the meat with exquisite spices that brought out the flavor of the game. Add in stewed dried vegetables and fresh sourdough bread, and he turned a simple camp meal into something even Deborah couldn't match.

On the fifth day after we left the National Road, Luc sat next to me while we broke our fast. We really hadn't spoken much since the morning the Duke of Standora arrived in Orrin. He was taking things slowly with our relationship as I had asked.

"Sounds like you're getting along well with the other clergy," he murmured.

"Through the last year, I've started getting to know them." I smiled. "Which I believe was your original recommendation when I was sentenced to the seat of Balance."

"You took my advice?" he said with mock dismay. "You never take my advice."

"Maybe the problem was how you present your advice," Migina said around a mouthful of bread.

Everyone in the camp turned and stared at the Conflict priestess. Her fellow Conflict priest Brother Piru nudged her foot with his.

She swallowed and shrugged. "I wasn't offering insult, High Brother. It's learning to communicate in the other person's way so they can understand."

"And you're an expert in not understanding how to communicate," Zihna teased the Conflict priestess.

"True," Migina admitted. "Especially not right after I wake regardless of the hour I do." She turned Luc. "I truly apologize, High Brother Luc."

"Apology accepted, Sister." Luc nodded. "It takes quite a bit before my hackles rise." He shot a mischievous expression in my direction before he turned back to Migina. "The chief justice is the one you need to watch out for."

A worried look filled Migina's face when she glanced at me. "I've never heard of the chief justice ordering lashes over an alleged insult."

"Oh, she wouldn't do that." Luc grinned. "She prefers her retaliation to be . . . more personal."

I groaned. "Oh, Balance. Are you still whining about that snake in your bedroll? That was eight summers ago!"

The junior clergy weren't sure if they should laugh until High

Brother Ben roared. Then the entire group followed, including the wardens, peacekeepers and support staff.

"So Warden Gina," Ben said. "What does she do to you and your fellows if you step out of line?"

"Oh, she constantly threatens to behead us," Gina said cheerily. "But I'd take that over a snake in my bedroll any day." She mock shuddered.

I rolled my eyes while everyone laughed at my expense.

Some instinct teased the edge of my mind, and I looked behind us. All too familiar swirls of purple, pink and red accented by flashes of white colored the clouds to the west. My heart beat a staccato rhythm in my chest and blood roared in my ears. We were half a night's ride to the next campsite.

"We've got a problem," I murmured.

"What?" Migina looked over her shoulder.

"There's a storm building behind us."

Luc called a halt to our march. *What do you see?*

He must have picked up on my unease. He'd learned to listen to me during our years on circuit when it came to weather. I could often see the change in air temperatures long before the signs were visible to humans with normal eyesight.

I nudged Nassa up to Luc. "There's a massive thunderstorm building behind us."

His brow creased. "How far?"

"Roughly five leagues," I answered. "So far the lightning is staying in the clouds, but with the rise of hot air, it won't be long before it's hitting the ground."

Luc cursed. "And no cover out here." He looked at the surrounding terrain.

Sisquoc padded over to our horses in his panther form. *We need to get to the next rise. This section of the desert is known for flash flooding.* I relayed his words.

"But the rise will make us vulnerable to the lightning," Ben said.

I could feel everyone's attention on me. "I haven't been able to replicate what happened during the summer, much less tried to control natural lightning. I don't know if I could do anything."

"Personally, I'd rather die instantly from a lightning strike than drown slowly in a flood," Brother Teluhci of Thief said.

"Let's pick up our pace, people!" Luc called out.

Thank the Twelve, it was night. Our people and mounts couldn't have kept the clip he set for long in the desert's daytime heat.

We didn't stop for our usual Second Night meal break. We didn't have time with the storm gaining on us. One of the Wilding wardens did pause long enough for Farrah to shift back to her human form and mount her own steed. Her short fox legs were a detriment at the speed we were going. Farrah and her warden easily caught up with us because even our horses seemed to sense the urgency to reach our goal.

A chill wind swept sand and dust into the air, and our group pull up their hoods. The first low rumble of thunder echoed across the basin we traversed. I watched over my shoulder for the next flash of lightning. When it appeared, I counted my heartbeats before the boom rebounded across the rocks and boulders.

Anthea? Luc didn't turn to look at me or use verbal speech. He would have gotten a mouthful of grit if he had.

A league and closing fast.

Everyone with silent speech join with those who don't, Luc ordered. *I know it's uncomfortable, but I don't want to lose anyone in this storm. Anthea?*

Claudia and I have the peacekeepers, I responded. *Claudia?*

I'm here, and I have my warden, she said. Our link strengthened as we both fed magic into it.

I gathered the four Balance wardens before I reached for the lead peacekeeper. *Leyti?*

Yes, m'lady? He had a tiny bit of unease, but that could have been from the oncoming storm as much as me touching his mind.

Talk to your people through me. I laughed. *I don't want to scare them more than I already do.*

I didn't interfere with, merely facilitated, Leyti's conversation with the other three peacekeepers. He explained what the Temple personnel were doing to keep everyone safe. DiCook had chosen his people well. None of them balked at what we asked. I thanked the Twelve for that small mercy, especially with the storm bearing down on us.

What passed for a path in the middle of the desert started to rise. Nassa snorted and huffed at the climb. I jerked as I spotted a large panther sitting on a boulder above us.

Sisquoc barked the harsh cough of the mountain cats at me, their version of laughter. The wind suddenly died. Ahead of us, clergy and wardens rigged the oiled leather of our tents into lean-tos over the upright boulders. It would provide us a little protection from the storm.

I dismounted and handed Nassa's reins to Gina before I climbed up the boulder to join Sisquoc. *We have everyone?*

Yes. He looked up at me. *I pray to the Twelve we are high enough.*

Did you want to shift back before the storm arrives?

Are you jesting? He shook his head. *Fur is much warmer than skin.* He looked to the west once again. *The night will be colder than usually after the storm passes, and a fire will be difficult to maintain. I hope Wildling will take pity on us.*

Brilliant purple-white split the sky half of a heartbeat before a peal of thunder deafened us. Then the deluge poured from the clouds.

Chapter 8

Sisquoc and I retreated to the shelter our companions had jury-rigged between boulders. The wind rose again and threatened to yank the stakes from the dampening soil. The heavy oiled leathers flapped as if they were condors attempting to take flight.

Our minuscule shelter and the boulders meant we weren't the tallest things on the rise. That gave the lightning other targets. However, I crouched down near the edge of the shelter to keep an eye on the spinning air above us. Waterspouts were known to come ashore during violent storms, and I'd heard tales of similar whirlwinds formed from dirt on the Great Plains. Here in the Valley of the Lost, there was very little plant life to hold down the dust until it was thoroughly soaked.

I thought sucking mud and flash flooding would be our next problem. Instead, hail the size of my fist struck the rocks. The balls of ice shattered, and splinters flew in every direction. Even the well-trained Temple mounts whinnied in terror.

The clergy and wardens worked to calm the horses, though the humans' anxiety pricked against my psyche. We couldn't afford to let the animals injure themselves or run away in this storm. Blue water swirled over yellow-green sand and around the purple hunks of hailstone.

Sisquoc padded over to sit next to me as the hailstones gave way to a torrent of water. He could see better with his panther eyes than regular humans. But I doubted even his sight could pierce the sheets of lilac rain any more than I could.

The water is starting to rise, he commented.

Yes. The section of the basin where we were when I first spotted the thunderstorm had already formed a small lake. *Have you been out in this part of the desert?*

A crack of thunder swallowed the coughing laugh of the Wildling priest. *Twice. Years ago with trade delegations. A place can change so much, and yet still be the same.*

Lightning flashed, and I counted again until the thunder rumbled. The sheets of rain faded to steady drops. *The storm is moving off.*

We will need to wait for the water to drain away. It appears to be a still pool, but it isn't, he said.

I know.

His curiosity scratched at my mind before he asked, *May I see through your eyes for a moment, Chief Justice?*

Certainly. I placed my right palm on his back and felt his sharp inhalation as our link became more intimate.

Sisquoc's breathing turned into a purr. *I never imagined so much color in the world.*

His statement prompted my own curiosity. *Humans can see in color. Granted it's not the same order of colors I perceive.*

Wildlings see the world how our second form would see it. Another coughing laugh. *Everything appears in shades of blue and green to me, and my night vision is excellent just like my brothers who were born as true panthers.*

I frowned as I considered his words. *But there are non-talents whose sight is also restricted. That was the subject of Master Healer Bly's research for her promotion in rank. She asked me to listen to her blasted speech and pick it apart for logical fallacies.*

Sisquoc grunted. *She used several of us in Wildling as additional test subjects.*

Your high brother let her?

He was fascinated by the analysis, Sisquoc said.

I chuckled. *The research or the healer doing the research?*

Yes. Another coughing laugh. *However, it was a fascinating test.*

A rumble that wasn't thunder interrupted our shared humor. With a sudden lunge, Sisquoc's claws pierced my robes and skin as he shoved me to the side. The two boulders on the west side of our little shelter fell away, dragging the tents with it. The patch of dirt where I had crouched a moment ago slid after the boulders.

Horses screamed and people shouted as more of the little rise on which we perched collapsed into the flash flood below us.

"Sisquoc!" I rolled onto stomach and grabbed the loose fur and skin on the back of his neck. He clawed at the soil, attempting to climb up. The Wildling was too damn big for me to drag to safety.

"Help me!" I screamed at instant before Sisquoc slid from my grasp. My heart froze in horror as he was swallowed by the turquoise sluice running down the side of the rise. "Sisquoc!"

Chapter 9

Gina dragged me from the western edge of the rise. "You can't follow him. With this rain, we'll lose you and anyone else who tries to go after him."

"He's still alive," I screamed. We were still linked intimately. I could feel the Wildling priest struggling to keep his head above the surface of the river of cold water, mud, and rocks.

"I believe you, but we can't afford to kill the entire group trying to rescue one person in a storm and flood," Gina yelled back.

Farrah, Claudia, and Migina approached, and I was ready to lash out at them.

"Where is he?" Farrah shouted over another rumble, which thank Balance was only thunder.

I pointed in Sisquoc's general direction. He was being swept toward the center of the growing lake.

"Can you time freeze the basin?" Claudia asked.

I stared at her like she'd gone mad. "The energy required—"

"Use the rest of us as extra power," Claudia said. "That will give Zihna, Migina and Farrah a chance to drag his ass back here."

"If I lose control before they get back—" I started.

Claudia grabbed my shoulders. "You won't. You're far more powerful than you realize. I have faith you can do this, Anthea." She swept her arm around us. "You have the surrounding hills and mountains to ground yourself. I know damn well you can do an outdoor rewind. That means you can do an outdoor freeze."

I nodded and sat on the ground. The chill from the damp soil and rocks penetrated my leather leggings, but I brushed the discomfort aside. Fear and excitement poked against my psyche as the word spread of our rescue attempt.

No, not attempt. Our rescue of Sisquoc.

We had to get him back. He'd fought renegades, skinwalkers, and demons for over a year. I couldn't let him die in a mudslide and flash flood.

Farrah had stripped already. She seized my face between her palms. Her mind melded with mine and Sisquoc. Zihna and Migina followed. Hands rested on each of my shoulders, and suddenly everyone was in my head. Clergy, wardens, peacekeepers, the handful of support staff.

I rested my hands on the damp rock, closed my eyes, and slowly exhaled. The whispered words of the spell raced along the rim of the basin before they turned inwards and swallowed the flood.

Everything stopped. The rain in the air. The frightened whinnies of our horses. With every human linked together, they were unaffected by the spell. The part of us that were Farrah, Migina, and Zihna scrambled down the south side of the escarpment and raced for the part of us that was Sisquoc.

Breathe, Anthea, Luc whispered in my mind. We all took a breath. Then another. Our legs pumped as we raced over the watery mud. Except it was getting harder to gulp in air. The mud encased our chest.

We were in the right location, but where were we? We put our nose to the jelly-like mud. Dead insects. A couple of scorpions. A drowned rattler. There. There was the scent of our panther self.

We found the right spot, our snout barely above the sluice dragging us into the frigid basin water. We collapsed on our knees and dug until we could see again. We concentrated, feeling around our body and gently tugged on our flesh.

The mud sucked our limbs. Sinews jerked, and bones wrenched. The pain was far worse than shifting our form. Wildling was not giving up His sacrifice willingly.

More digging with hands and paws. With a slurping sound, we were free of the mud river. We lay panting on the jelly for a moment before a trickle of sweat down our spine reminded us we needed to get out of the basin before we lost control of the time freeze spell.

We got to our feet and started running for the rise. Stitches in our sides from running a league could be ignored. The dislocated toe and the broken ribs sent sharp stabbing pains through us. Our head ached abominably from using our moving talent. Those faded within the rest of us. We had to get back to the rise.

When we fell, we threw our arm over our shoulder and hauled us to our feet. Our paws picked out a steady rhythm. Tension grew as we struggled up the escarpment. We lowered ropes to haul us to the top.

Once we were all safe, we let go of our spell. Rain splashed down as if thrown from buckets. The lightning no longer flashed directly overhead, and the thunder resembled snoring. Even the horses had quieted.

I blinked the water out of my eyes. Every muscle and joint were stiff from the effort to hold that large of space frozen long enough for the priestesses to pull Sisquoc free of the mud.

My body only gave me a moment of respite. Muscles cramped and twisted, and I cried out in agony.

"Anthea!" Claudia shrieked.

"Grab her waterskin. There's muscle relaxer and the pain powder in her right saddlebag," Luc ordered. His fingers kneaded my neck and shoulders.

"Should-should have—brought—healer," I forced out from between my clenched jaw.

"With our luck, the healer would have been the one swept away in the mudslide," he murmured as he worked. "And we wouldn't have been able to save them."

Someone pulled off my boots. Another person tried to straighten my right leg. I screamed at the unintentional torture.

"Not like that, Long Feather," Mylon snapped. "You'll tear her muscle fibers." Strong fingers massaged my left calf. "When the body contracts like that, you must coax it to relax. It's no different than breaking a horse."

More fingers dug into my right calf. A deep-throated chuckle bounced off the remaining boulders. "There you go. You need to get them to respond without actually breaking them if you know what I mean."

It was the longest speech I'd ever heard from Warden Mylon before. However, his hands were performing their own type of magic. The agony started to recede.

"Sisquoc?" I look up at Luc.

"The ladies dug him out." Luc's hands moved to my temples and scalp. "He dislocated a toe—"

"—and he has at least two broken ribs," I murmured. "I felt that through the link."

"And he swallowed some mud that he's already ejected from his stomach." Luc smiled. "Lady Alessa and Noemi are tending to him." Luc's smile faded. "Brother Piru has already scouted the other side of this rise. The water's just as deep and fast on that side. We'll be here at least through the coming day."

"Should have brought a weather oracle with us as well as a healer," I said.

"We had no reason to expect any storms, m'lady." Mylon had finished with my thigh muscles. He carefully straightened my left leg and began kneading my foot. "It's too early in the season." He made a disgusted sound in the back of his throat. "Hogarth is right. This winter will be worse than the last."

Claudia crouched next to Luc. "Open your mouth, Anthea."

He propped me up enough I could swallow doses of the pain powder and muscle relaxer she gave me along with a healthy drink of water to wash the bitter taste from my tongue.

"How's Zihna?" I asked.

Claudia chuckled. "Already asleep. She has a small moving talent, which is convenient when you leave your shoes on the other side of the room. Shifting that much mud and Wildling nearly burned her out."

"Tell her thank you," I murmured. "To all of them for working as fast as they did. I couldn't bear losing any more friends."

Claudia laughed again. "We're fond of you as well, Anthea."

My eyes closed as Luc and my wardens continued their ministrations on my limbs. The last thing I remember was Luc softly singing Light's morning salutation.

Chapter 10

I woke to the soft murmur of more than two voices, which was odd. I was usually the first one awake. My mouth tasted bitter and dry. I pushed up on my elbows.

"Good eventide, sleepyhead," Luc teased.

I blinked as memory caught up with my consciousness. Last night's events seemed like some horrible nightmare. "What hour is it?"

"A candlemark after First Evening," he said.

I bolted upright. "We should be on the road by now."

He placed his hand on my shoulder. "The mud from last night's storm is still too thick for us to make the next waystation before dawn. Not to mention, everyone in our party has a bit of a magic hangover from your spell. One extra day spent here isn't going to kill us."

Everyone close enough to hear Luc stared at him.

"I meant it figuratively," he growled.

Ben crossed our little campsite and sat down on my left side. "Luc is right. This type of travel is hard enough." He lowered his voice. "I am concerned about Sisquoc's broken ribs. They weren't knocked out of place, but it wouldn't take much to do so out here. I did give him a drop of soma tears to deal with the pain."

"If he punctures a lung before we reach Diné, he may not survive," I said.

"Luckily, Wildlings heal much faster than the rest of us." Ben smiled. "He considers his injuries a fair trade for your life."

I knew Ben's jest was intended to get me to laugh, but it only added to my pile of guilt. I started to rub my face when I realized my hands were covered in cracked and dried mud. "How bad is our supply situation?"

"We lost two tents and the saddlebags from one of Ademaro's supply horses," Luc reported. "We still have enough food since Sisquoc and Farrah have been hunting for us. Overall, we were damn lucky last night. The entire rise could have given way."

That meant we hadn't lost the dispatches from Queen Teodora to the Matriarch. I wasn't sure if the luck was the blessing it appeared to be.

I picked off the dried mud from my hands. The rest of me was just as filthy. I longed for my bathing pool back in Orrin, knowing full well it was foolish of me to do so. For someone whose father grew up in this area of the world, I sorely detested the desert, especially after last night's misadventures.

Ademaro made up for our misery with a delightfully seasoned dished made from dried and powdered potatoes, bacon, and herbs. It was filling and far better tasting than jerky and hardtack in the saddle.

Afterwards, people told stories, sang, or played a Jing game with small pieces of thick paper Shi Hua had introduced to the Orrin clergy. She called the pieces cards, but the game itself was called Leaf. Unfortunately, since their designs were in ink, I couldn't read them to play.

I gazed out over the basin we'd crossed last night. The surface water was gone, and to me, the sand and dirt looked as it had before the storm hit us.

"Are you thinking of going back?" Migina approached and stood next to me.

I turned my attention back to the desert. "No. I was actually contemplating how to use a flash flood against a demon army."

She grunted in surprise. "Do you ever stop thinking about them?"

"Not since they knocked me out and chained me in the DiRoy manse last year." I chuckled. "So to answer your next question, my obsession with demons is one of the many topics High Sister Mya covers with me during our meetings."

"I wasn't going to pry . . . that deeply anyway." Migina flashed a wry smile. "I do apologize for stepping out of line with you. I thought the rumors spread about you and High Brother Luc were just that. Nasty little rumors."

"There is a certain irony when someone who means to lie accidentally tells the truth," I murmured.

Migina laughed. "Honestly, I think the restrictions regarding your Temples are rather stupid."

"They are there for a reason." I inhaled deeply. The air was already returning to the acrid taste in the back of my throat. "I don't think I really understood the necessity for them until the edict came down."

"You do know that Claudia has no interest in Luc, don't you?" Migina asked softly.

"It was a little hard to miss everyone's personal feelings when we were linked together last night," I said sourly. "You know you could simply tell Zihna how you feel instead of constantly tormenting her."

"Where's the fun in that?" Migina replied.

"How does High Brother Han deal with such impertinence?"

"Well, if you decide to you need to teach me a lesson, I'd be happy to be your sparring partner sometime," Migina said.

"No," I shook my head at her flirtatious behavior. "That's not a place you want to go."

"Then I truly do owe you amends, Chief Justice."

"You already repaid any debt to me by rescuing Sisquoc from the mudslide."

She started and glanced over at the Wildling priest. When she looked at me, her right eyebrow rose.

"No, his heart is definitely committed to High Brother Aduba, formerly of Tandor."

She chuckled. "Then I shall leave you to your thoughts while I'm behind, m'lady." She drifted back toward the fire. Without us traveling during the night, the chill air was slightly more uncomfortable.

"Is everything all right, m'lady?" Long Feather asked.

"Yes. Why?" And why in Balance's name was everyone checking on me?

"May I speak freely, m'lady?"

"Yes." My curiosity was getting the better of me.

"We've never seen you this jovial with members of the other temples," he answered.

I snorted. "Little Bear told you to make sure I was polite to the others, didn't he?"

"He did mention such a concern to Gina." Humor laced Long Feather's voice. "But since she and Dezba are busy upholding Balance's honor in a game of Mill, I presumed to check on you. If I've stepped out of line, I beg your forgiveness."

"No." I shook my head. "There's nothing for you to ask forgiveness for. I don't exactly trust myself right now. The queen believes this diplomatic mission was important enough to send me. I pray I deserve her trust."

Long Feather glanced over his shoulder at the rest of our group before he turned back to me and lowered his voice. "This is no normal trade or diplomatic delegation. I understand the myriad reasons why you cannot be forthcoming to us, but as your wardens, we trust you will inform us of what observations and precautions you may need."

I cocked my head. "Did Gina put you up to interrogating me?"

"No, m'lady. However, it has been a subject of discussion amongst the four of us." He touched on the very issue that bothered me.

I groaned. "By Balance, I would tell all of you if I knew what was really going on."

"That's what were feared," he said.

"What do you mean?" I asked quietly.

Once again he checked to see if anyone was paying attention to our conversation. "The spy within Balance could have put something in the dispatches you are to deliver that may be detrimental to your health."

I frowned. "I'm not the person . . ."

Balance, I was getting slow. There were so many ways the renegades could scheme to have me beheaded by the Diné. I cursed under my breath.

Finally, I looked up at Long Feather. "Why didn't one of you bring this up earlier?"

He sighed. "Gina was sure you would tell us once we were clear of any ears you couldn't trust."

We were both silent for a long moment, staring at the expanse of desert. "If the four of you want to go home, you have my permission."

He chuckled. "The Temples do not work that way, m'lady."

"I can write a message to Yanaba, Elizabeth, and Little Bear."

Long Feather laughed even louder. "Sivan's the one we truly fear if we fail to bring you back intact."

Even I had to chuckle at his observation. So I needed to stay alive in order to protect my wardens from my chief of household's wrath. A year and a half ago, I wouldn't have considered such an action.

Maybe everyone was right about me changing. I hoped it was for the better.

Otherwise, the demons may have planted an alternate personality in me. One that would betray my people at the worst possible moment.

If so, it would drive me to revenge their deaths at an obscene cost. I sent a silent prayer to Balance to help me figure out this puzzle before it drove me mad.

Once again, I received no answer from Her.

Chapter 11

We resumed our travels the following sundown. To my surprise, plants were sprouting nearly everywhere. I looked around us, not paying any attention whatsoever to the trail. Luckily, Nassa was smart enough to stick to the vague path, even if the horses in front of her thought to veer from it.

"I never realized how much life is in the desert," I said.

"High Brother Ben's practically dancing in his saddle." Claudia laughed. "With such an early rain, he'll be able to collect some rare plants and roots."

"He's not planning to drag them all the way to Diné and back, is he?" I stared at the priestess.

"First of all, we have an extra horse now." Claudia grinned. "Second, he'll be able to trade with their Vintner clergy for things they have that we don't."

I nodded. It made sense to trade while we could. Without Tandor as a way stop, it would be harder to travel the Valley of the Lost except in deep winter.

Claudia shook her head. She appeared to enjoy the night through her haphazard curls. "Thank you for allowing me to come with you."

"Well, there were official reasons—" I started.

"No, I mean it's nice not to have to wear my veil all the time and pretend everything is all right."

I examined at her more closely. "Have you talked to—"

"The High Sister insisted," Claudia bit out. "My veil doesn't block everyone's damn looks of pity. And everyone expected me to break before you did."

"It's not a contest," I murmured.

"I know." She sighed. "I just needed to get away for a while. That's all. You can't tell me staying at Child for the last two months was a lark for you."

"No, it definitely wasn't," I said dryly. "Did you know High Mother Leocadia has a bit of Light talent, too?"

Claudia nodded. "And none of the four children she's born has a lick of it. She visited with me at the Healers Guild while I was recovering. Inheriting talent can still be a throw of Thief's dice."

"How would you feel if you transferred to Light?" I asked.

"The likelihood of that happening . . ." She stared at me. "You're serious, aren't you?"

"Sister Shi Hua has shown me some of Issuran rules for clergy are illogical," I said. "This edict wouldn't have been necessary if we cultivated anyone with Light talent, not just men."

Claudia glanced at the head of our column before she returned her attention to me. "How does our current high brother of Light feel about woman in his ranks? Because he was rather forced to accept Sister Shi Hua."

Her point had been something I'd been mulling over since we'd left Orrin. I understood why the heads of the Jing Temples of Balance and Light agreed to Shi Hua's temporary transfer. They wanted closer ties with our Temples. Besides, she was already here.

But what made the Issuran heads agree? My own Reverend Mother knew Shi Hua was a distance speaker. If the Reverend Mother was a renegade as we suspected, why in Balance would she concur with my recommendation?

We already knew Reverend Father Farrell of Light didn't approve of the way my Reverend Mother dealt with my illegal execution of Samael DiRoy. Not to mention, he was worried a vote of no confidence would be called among the Light high brothers over the infiltration of his order by the renegades, and Luc would be nominated to replace him.

What if Farrell were actually a renegade himself? That would mean his real issue with Reverend Mother Alara was she kept me alive.

"Anthea?" Claudia said.

I realized I hadn't answered her question. "As long as everyone performs their duties in his Temple, I don't believe he cares what's between their legs."

"That's not what was rolling around inside your skull," she murmured.

"Are we still linked?" I teased.

"I don't need to be linked with someone to read their facial expression." She was quiet for a moment before she added, "My own high sister and I are worried about why the queen is sending you and High Brother Luc on this diplomatic mission instead of a trusted royal like one of her younger daughters."

"You're not the only ones," I said.

"So what do we do?"

"Pray the Twelve don't bend us over a barrel," I said sourly.

Claudia slapped a hand over her mouth in an attempt to rein in her humor, but in the end, her laughter pealed across the desert night.

Chapter 12

Four nights later, Farrah met a Diné Wildling while she scouted ahead of the point riders. He changed from his coyote form into his human form to greet our party. Gina translated for us.

Apparently, my birth father insisted on sending out a scouting party after too-early-for-the-season thunderstorms moved through their territory. We explained to the Diné Wildling we had to wait out some flooding which delayed us for a day and a half.

He nodded. "You were wise to do so, but after what happened to the clergy who escaped from the demon consorts in Tandor, the Matriarch and our Reverend Parents feared you may have encountered something worse in your travels," he said through Gina.

"One of our party was injured in a mudslide," Luc said. "I know it's an imposition, but may we consult with a healer as to his injuries?"

"We are here to serve." The Diné Wildling bowed before he shifted back into his canine form and raced out into the desert. Farrah trotted after him.

"I do not need special treatment, High Brother," Sisquoc said mildly once the other two Wildlings were out of earshot.

"If that were true, you'd be sleeping better," Luc pointed out. The Wildling priest had accidentally shifted back to his human form in his sleep. He'd roused our entire camp with his cries of pain. However, reclining on saddlebags while in human form allowed him a little more rest.

"Besides," Luc added. "I'm sure the Diné Healers Guild will be happy with a share of the plants we collected on the way."

"Yes, High Brother." If Sisquoc dropped his argument so quickly, he was hurting a lot more than the hints of pain that intruded the other clergy's sleep.

We continued to the next campsite. Our maps and information from the Temple of Knowledge indicated a tiny pool fed by a spring. The thunderstorms in the area turned the spring into a gush of water spilling from the rocks. Nassa and the other horses took long drinks of the slightly muddy water of the pool. The rest of us filled our water skins from the natural spout formed by the extra rain.

At this point, we were all so weary no one wanted any food. Ademaro actually looked relieved he didn't have to perform his duties this morning. I stretched out between Gina and Dezba and tried to sleep through the heat of the day.

Apparently, I succeeded because next thing I knew someone touched my shoulder. My fingers curled around my dagger under my rolled cloak I used as a pillow. I looked up to see Long Feather with his forefinger over his lips.

I nodded and carefully got to my feet in order not to disturb my companions. Long Feather led me away from the sleepers to where Warden Jocasta and Claudia watched the horizon. I saw immediately why my own warden woke me.

A thin yellowish column rose into the sky. It wasn't the normal updrafts from the rocks and soil baking in the desert heat.

"Smoke?" I asked.

"Dust," Jocasta murmured.

"Riders," Claudia added.

"The Diné Wildling probably met with his people's outriders," Long Feather said.

"The distance-view glasses?" I asked.

"Too much dust for me to see anything specific." However, Jocasta handed the slender metal tube to me.

I examined the area and picked out a section of rock I could climb. Long Feather followed me to the top. I peered through the distance-viewer toward the dust rising from the horizon. Thank Balance, there was no horrid black line between the ground and the dust cloud the approaching riders kicked up.

Unless I was very wrong, and the demons wore human skins.

But would a demon allow another demon to ride it? The beasts had longer necks and bigger hooves than horses. I couldn't see any camel cooperating with a demon. The desert creatures barely tolerated humans riding on their backs.

I handed the distance-viewer to Long Feather. "Have you ever heard of demons riding each other?"

He shook his head and gazed through the tube. "Humans and camels. Still too far to see symbols, but the colors are predominantly dark red and gray." He shrugged and looked at me. "If the Reverend Father of Conflict was worried about us as their Wildling said, then he was already heading this way."

"I hope that's all it is," I muttered. "But let's wake the camp anyway. Just in case."

Thank the Twelve, my precaution was unnecessary.

When they arrived, the Diné Conflict wardens formed two solid ranks between us and their Reverend Father. His camel knelt. Then he pushed his way on foot to the head of the column. A brilliant grin lit his face.

"It is good to see you again, Chief Justice," he said in Issuran.

"A pleasure to see you also, Reverend Father," I replied in Diné as I inclined my head.

"You've been learning." His tone was even more pleased that his expression.

"Warden Gina will tell you my accuracy leaves something to be desired," I said wryly. "Father." I made a point of using the personal inflection.

He shrugged. "I wasn't sure how you would react. Things were not good between your mother and your predecessors. I didn't know what you'd been told."

"We'll talk about family after we get the business out of the way." I smiled and switched back to Issuran. "If I may introduce the rest of my party, Reverend Father."

We went through introductions before the Diné watered their camels. It was past First Afternoon, so the Reverend Father saw his people settled to nap. The rest of my own party did the same. Dezba had the afternoon watch. She took charge of the sentries for both sets of riders.

The Reverend Father joined me in my tent, which was now pitched slightly apart from the sleepers so we could talk. I'd rolled up three of the sides to gain whatever breeze I could while blocking the heat from the sun as it started its downward slide.

Luc and Ben made a point of taking seats on the ground sheet with us. I couldn't deny them since this was technically a diplomatic mission, but I was disappointed not to talk to my birth father privately.

I wasn't sure what exactly I wanted to say to him. Or even how to approach the subject of Gerd. But I didn't want to do any of it in front of Luc, much less Ben.

The Reverend Father greeted Luc as if he were an old friend. Yet, he was almost equally cordial to Ben. After asking how the citizens of Tandor were faring, he said, "Hogarth mentioned in his last letter he told you everything."

I nodded.

"Would you mind allowing me to use your public name, sir?" Luc grinned. "Since you are not my birth father."

"Kilchii."

I choked on the mouthful of water I'd taken from my skin. Somehow, I managed not to spray it all over the men.

Ben frowned. "Wait. What?"

The Reverend Father pounded on my back while I coughed to clear the water from my windpipe.

Luc clarified, "Reverend Father Kilchii is Anthea's birth father."

"Oh." Ben's eyes widened, but he made no further comment. Part of me wondered what he thought, but his shields leaked no emotion whatsoever.

I wiped the tears from my face, cleared my throat, and eyed my father. "Red Boy? Not even Red Man?"

He shrugged and smiled. "I was the smallest child in my novice class. I didn't go through my final growth spurt until after I was ordained. So the name stuck. And I use it as a reminder to my order not to underestimate any foe."

"Names aside, we are a little curious as to why your Matriarch asked for the chief justice and me specifically," Luc said.

The Reverend Father's smile faded. "Your queen, our Matriarch, and the headman of the Cliffdwellers each have a personal distance speaker. So did the king of Cant until his distance speaker died of what appeared to be a heart seizure three winters ago."

"And you suspect the Cant royal distance speaker's death was not from natural causes?" I asked.

"No one did before now," my father said grimly. "Queen Teodora's distance speaker was assassinated a month ago."

Luc and I exchanged looks before he said, "We were not aware of his death, sir."

"It is my understanding the queen is keeping it quiet," my father said.

"But why?" Ben asked.

"Because the skinwalkers and demons were trying to sow dissension between Cant and Issura last winter by raiding villages along the border." I twisted my fingers in my robes in an attempt to rein in my temper. "Without his distance speaker, it's more time-consuming to contact a neighboring ruler in order to solve a problem."

"It turned out to be a strategic mistake," my father commented. "The king of Cant called his people to arms so they were ready when the demon army appeared."

"But not before, he lost Rambla," I murmured.

"True," my father conceded with a nod. "However, our own Reverend Mother of Thief and I have been speaking with our counterparts in Issura through the Matriarch's distance speaker." He shook his head. "We believe the Issuran assassination is another attempt to disrupt communications between nations. They asked who the Matriarch would trust. I recommended you and Luc after seeing how the two of you responded to the problems in Tandor."

"While I appreciate your confidence in us, didn't they tell you that both the Temples of Balance and Light in Issura have been infiltrated?" Luc said.

My father nodded again. "The Duke of Standora believed your superiors would agree to this trip to either keep you safe or get you out of their way." He eyed Ben. "I'm glad you have someone of your rank to accompany you, and keep you out of trouble."

"The spy within Balance may have influenced Reverend Mother Alara to send Anthea for a different reason." Ben looked at me. "What if the renegades believe their plot to manipulate you into demon influence succeeded?"

Bile rose in my throat. "It makes the most sense out of all the possibilities we've discussed along our trip."

Luc cursed softly in Cantan.

"What are you talking about?" My father asked.

I ran my dry tongue over my equally dry lips. "It's a long story, but the gist is Gerd became a skinwalker, and I fell under demon influence."

Chapter 13

My father's mouth dropped open, and he stared at me for a very long time before he said, "Is she dead?"

I nodded and swallowed hard. I didn't want to answer him, but he deserved to know the rest of the truth, no matter how bad it made me appear to him. "I beheaded her myself."

He released a deep breath. "I'm so sorry you were put in that position, Anthea. I never wanted that for you." Sorrow rolled off him in waves. "I thought—I hoped Thalia and Hogarth were exaggerating her behavior. If anything, they understated the situation." He looked back up at me. "By the Twelve, I should never have left Issura all those years ago."

"You never had a choice," I said softly. "If you and Gerd had run away together, you both would have been hunted down."

"But you wouldn't have been forced into Balance."

I laughed. "Bad decisions run through my entire maternal line."

He glanced at Luc before his attention returned to me. "Some decisions within the family are better than others."

I don't know why his approval of Luc mattered to me, but it did. "You're right. We made three good choices."

Ben remained silent through the whole exchange, but it wasn't like no one in Orrin knew my personal history. Not when I announced the truth at High Brother Kam's funeral.

"And this demon influence?" Father asked softly.

My mouth was drier than the sand beneath the ground cloth we sat upon. But before I could gather my wits to answer him, Ben spoke.

"Say nothing, Anthea," the High Brother of Vintner said. "How we handle issues in Orrin is no one else's business."

"You think I would behead my own daughter?" Father stared aghast at Ben.

"I know how things can be twisted," Ben said. "Gerd isn't the only one who's used Anthea to further their own ends. Both Reverend Mother Alara and Queen Teodora manipulated the law to keep Anthea alive and free in order to use her for their own purposes. And Gerd cast a demon spell upon me, one to control me, force me to kill Anthea. I do not mean to personally insult you, Reverend Father, but I have little trust for anyone's motives other than our chief justice and high brother of Light these days."

The corners of my father's mouth quirked. "When it comes to anyone from Issura, neither do I, High Brother."

"Wonderful," I quipped. "Everyone trusts Luc and me, but they're doing everything possible to trick us into mistrusting each other."

My father cocked his head. "What are you talking about?"

Luc and I stared at each other for a long moment. We'd worked together for so long, knew each other so well, silent speech wasn't always necessary. He gave the slightest of nods.

"Luc and I were deliberately matched for a circuit team in the hope we would develop romantic feelings for each other." I swallowed hard. "Then, we were sent to the circuit of Eastern Orrin, one of the most isolated circuits in the queendom . . . until they were ready for us."

"Ready for you?" Father asked. "For what purpose?"

"To corrupt us." Luc grimaced. "We think the renegades have been working on a plan for decades. Possibly longer."

"The demons don't think like we do." I shook my head. "Despite their numbers their strengths, and their powers, we've held our own against their invasions because they cannot anticipate our tactics, and they need one of us to bind them to this plane of existence."

"However, they are adapting," Luc said. "They've discovered if their children are hatched on this plane, those demons cannot be banish back to their own dimension."

"Even worse, the renegades and the Assassins Guild have been teaching the demons how we think, how we act, how humans work together," I added. "And they are all using that knowledge against us."

Father was silent for a very long time. I couldn't hear anything beyond the roaring of my ears. He seemed to approve of Luc, but I literally admitted our affair pre-dated the edict for Balance and Light to procreate. Would he chose duty over practicality?

"And this demon influence?" Father finally asked.

I sagged. "I had a demon grimoire in my possession. And only mine."

He frowned as he regarded me, then Luc, and finally Ben. "Who are you three trying to protect?"

"They had nothing to do with the grimoire, Reverend Father Kilchii," I said in Diné with the appropriate formal inflection.

A sharp spike of anger thrust into my psyche. "Are you two such cowards you would let a comrade sacrifice herself without a word from either of you?" he spat in Issuran at the men.

"You're the one who asked if we believed you would kill your own daughter in the line of duty," Luc said. "You have your answer."

"Did you willingly acquire this grimoire?" Father asked.

"Yes," I replied.

He groaned. "I may not be trained in logic as you have, Anthea, but even I can tell you are only speaking part of the truth. I cannot help you without knowing everything. As long as you haven't joined the renegades, I don't care what you've done." He eyed Luc and Ben. "Any of you."

"To win at any cost?" I asked bitterly.

"Sometimes there are no good solutions," Father answered. "Sometimes, the best you can do is minimize the damage." A sad look crossed his face. "I thought you learned that lesson in Tandor. You chose to save the populace. Yet, you left a blind spot in Issura's southern defenses."

My blood thrummed at his insult. "Do you believe I purposely weakened my queendom's defenses? If you thought that, why didn't you say something six months ago?"

"Because I agreed with your choice, Anthea," Father said softly. "I'm merely pointing out you are not looking at all alternatives now."

"I am," I snapped. "The single penalty for possession of a demon grimoire is death."

"When you found the demon grimoire in Sister Gretchen's saddlebag, did you behead Sister Dragonfly because she unwittingly possessed the grimoire in the bag? When you turned over the grimoire to Reverend Mother Alara, did she behead you?" He shook his head. "There are exceptions than simple possession in order for justice to be preserved. If your colleagues believed you were worth saving, doesn't that say more about their moral code than your alleged guilt?"

"You're making an emotional plea, Reverend Father," I bit out. "And this isn't about my alleged guilt. This is about saving my friends. I will not let the renegades' tricks be used to harm them."

He leaned back and regarded me. "You've changed."

"Demons in my head and a two-month stint in the care of Child will do that for a person," I said more calmly. I couldn't read my birth father. Not the way I could other people. It was almost as if he were a quicksilver like High Brother Talbert or Reverend Father Biming. However, I could sense his presence where Talbert or Biming didn't seem to exist. I waited to see his reaction.

"High Brother Ben said they wanted to use you against us," he said gently. "Me personally or Diné as a nation?"

I blew out a deep breath. "Considering Gerd was also used to influence me, I would have to say both."

"Anthea, please tell me what happened to you." Father held out both hands, palms up and fingers spread. "I swear it won't go further than me."

"But you could be truthspelled," I pointed out.

"Even you have to admit, a truthspell is only as affective as the questions that are asked." His wry smile melted something inside me. My father's sense of humor was so similar to Luc's. Is that part of the reason I fell in love with him? Yet, I didn't meet my birth father until this spring. Thirty-one winters after I was born. Ten winters after Luc and I became lovers.

"Tell him," Luc said softly. "He needs to know what kind of tricks to watch for."

I turned to Ben.

He frowned. "It's not my life I'm concerned about, Anthea, but—" He released a deep breath. "I will abide by your decision. You both know Reverend Father Kilchii better than I do."

Slowly, hesitantly, I told my father of the events of the last few months. Gerd's escape from the Temple of Balance in Standora. Her return to Orrin. The murder of Dragonfly's head of household Gregorios. The spell she cast on Ben to use him to kill me. The kidnappings of Claudia and Luc. The death of their son.

Everything, including my seizure of the grimoire and how it affected me. How one of the Balance squires found her talent and saved the other. How she saved me.

When I finished, the slight breeze felt less hot, and members of both parties stirred in the joint campsite. I waited for my birth father to say something.

Anything.

He released a deep breath and shook his head. "No wonder they want you dead." He looked at me. "Not only can you see demons, you possessed that cursed tome twice and still managed to fight its influence." Slowly, a smile spread across his face. "You will need to share this tale with the Matriarch and the heads of our Temples. And, Anthea?"

"Yes, sir?" I said.

"You have nothing to fear from the Diné nation. Anyone who can stand against skinwalkers has our utmost respect."

Chapter 14

Now that we knew we would cross the Diné border tonight, it didn't take the Issuran contingent long to pack and load their gear. Excitement ran through both groups, but it probably had more to do with the upcoming holiday after the Day of Death plus visitors this late after a very bad trading season. According to Ben, the last vestiges of the sun's light shone when we started on the road.

We passed beneath the arch symbolizing our entry into Diné as the waning moon peeked above the mountains. An eagle perched on the arch's crest. Wildling magic brushed along my skin.

"You're staring, Anthea," Ben murmured.

I chuckled. "I can't help it. If the Twelve had given me a choice, I would have been a Wildling with the second form of a bird. Flying would be the ultimate joy to me."

He laughed at my whimsical fantasy. "Even with lice and fleas?"

"Maybe not with those," I admitted. "I'd still want a warm bath in which to preen my feathers."

"I can't imagine being in a different Temple," he mused. "But if I were, I'd rather be in Light or Love. I'd want to bring people joy."

With the easy camaraderie we'd developed on this journey, I decided to take a chance. "May I ask you a personal question, High Brother?"

He flashed a wry grin before he said, "As long as I have the opportunity to forgo answering it."

"Very well." I regarded Ben. "Are you Lady Katarina's birth father?"

He chuckled. "First of all, it's impolite for someone to ask such a thing of a Spring Ritual child. But since you know who your birth father is, no, I didn't socialize with Sister Ilina until after Katarina's third winter. In addition, the lady has Sister Ilina's blue eyes and blond hair."

It meant Katarina's birth father probably had the same coloring as Ilina. Some people put an emphasis on those colors of eyes and skin since they were rare in the world. It made me glad everyone looked the same to my odd sight.

"I hear," I murmured. "Forgive my curiosity, High Brother."

"Never apologize for curiosity," he said. "I know you didn't mean your question to be cruel. However, may I ask the reason for the question?"

"Meeting Katarina set me on my current path," I said. "I care about her. And as I've gotten to know you, I realize how many qualities you share. Kindness. Empathy. Level-headedness. I guess I want to find her birth father because she misses her mother so much."

"Thank you for the compliments," he replied. "It makes me wish I truly were the lady's father."

"Have you talked with Katarina about Ilina?" I asked softly.

"I—no," he admitted. "I didn't want to impose. It's not like Ilina and I were open about our feelings for each other though our relationship was hardly a secret."

"Lady Katarina is a highly intelligent woman." I smiled at Ben. "I'm sure she knew and was trying to respect the personal space Sister Ilina carved out for herself."

"Most likely," he agreed.

"Plus, you would have someone who shares your grief," I said. "And so would she."

"I . . . will take your suggestion under consideration," he replied. "May I ask how much of this is from High Sister Mya?"

"None of it." When I glanced at Ben, his right eyebrow was raised. I chuckled. "Actually, the high brother of Light pointed out I wouldn't have had half the troubles I did if I made more of an effort to understand and get to know my fellow seats."

"That's wise counsel," he murmured. "What took you so long to follow it?"

I sighed at his gentle poke. "That's where Mya's assistance became invaluable. I needed to stop carrying my past. It weighted every emotion. Every decision. I wasn't truly being objective outside of the courtroom. I . . . hope her counseling makes me a better justice."

"You have always been an excellent justice." Ben smiled at me. "Your issue has been you believe you're the only one who can save the world."

I considered his words. Mya had said something similar during our talks. Luc had warned me my behavior verged on arrogance when I didn't socialize with my fellow seats. I needed to do better. Maybe Ben accompanying us on this trip turned into more of an opportunity than a burden.

As we rode through the desert night, he told me Master Healers Bly and Devin had been consulting with Ben and his clergy over various poisons and medicines. They continued to put together a master record specifically indexed for Balance investigations into questionable deaths.

I explained the weapons' index Master Bly's apprentice Simi was constructing. Ben was fascinated by the crossover of the Temples, Guilds, and the civilian government. I mentioned Chief Healer Aaron's suggestion of creating a new Guild that would assist the Temple of Balance in their investigations.

"I doubt the Temple of Death would go along with such an idea," Ben murmured. "Their leadership is still bitter over the healers creating their own guilds. And while I know your dedication to a thorough investigation in a suspicious death, their order is rather conservative in their views."

"But how much of our system for doing things is forgotten tradition?" I waved my left hand. "The swift disposal of corpses is necessary to prevent the demons from using them against us, but how many humans have gotten away with murder because of those customs?"

"Do you really believe someone would do such a thing?" Ben's right eyebrow rose again.

"After seeing what was done to Sister Gretchen and several Orrin children, I believe humans may be far worse than demons." I sighed. "I've never seen a demon turn on one of their own, and from my research, no one else has either."

"That's a rather grim assessment," Ben said.

"What's a grim assessment?" Migina asked as she rode up to my right.

"Our chief justice is comparing human morals to demon morals," Ben said.

That statement started a debate among our fellow travelers that lasted until we reached our next campsite at First Morning.

Chapter 15

The last night of our ride, Diné travelers joined our procession. Most were coming down out of the Gray Mountains with their flocks of sheep and goats. Others were artisans bringing their wares to sell at festivities in the Diné capital of Heart.

Or rather that's what the Diné name for Ajéí translated into Issuran. Heart wasn't a large city like Standora or Orrin. Few people lived there year round. Heart was more a collection of buildings that sat on a mesa overlooking the Red River and the Diné crop fields. Its essential function was a defensive spot on Diné wintering grounds at the edge of the Valley of the Lost.

Reverend Father Kilchii deliberately slowed our pace for those travelers on foot or with slower livestock. His care for his people made me respect him more than I had before. And we would still reach our destination before Second Morning.

When the sun peeked over the mountains at First Morning, everyone broke out singing the morning prayer. I could pick out Issuran, Diné, the Peaceful Sea trade tongue, and two Plains Nations languages. They blended together in a glorious hymn to Light.

For the first time since I left my circuit, I felt content.

As we got closer to Heart, we passed farmers in the fields, harvesting the last of their crops. They called out to the Diné Temple members surrounding the Issuran contingent, who responded jovially. Part of me regretted I could only make out a few words of what was said.

I leaned closer to Gina riding on my left. "What are they saying about Tandor?"

"The red-eyed Demon Slayer of Tandor has come to pay her respects to the Matriarch." Gina's grin was so wide it threatened to split her face in half.

"What?"

Long Feather eyed me from my right. "We're aware you don't like the attention, but with all due respect, Chief Justice, take the songs about the battle with good grace. We don't want to offend our hosts."

A flicker of unease spread through me. "Songs? What songs?"

"The Diné used oral histories and songs long before they adapted the Phoenician alphabet," Gina said. "The Elders have kept the tradition going because it's a method of respect." She narrowed her eyes. "And you will accept that respect, Chief Justice."

Ben's sharp remark from the night before last still bothered me though what he said was true. Even though I was within my rights to punish my wardens for their impertinence, I held my tongue. I brought Gina and Long Feather on this trip for their knowledge of Diné culture. However, it was bitter medicine to swallow, and I pulled my hood down as far as I could. This was supposed to be a diplomatic mission. Besides, why were civilians singing songs about me?

They should be telling heroic tales about their own people. Like the Comanche sortie that split the demons attention from the Issuran army. Or Reverend Father Kilchii's brilliant defense of the city. The combined Diné, Cliffdweller, and Plains Nations army saved our hides from the demons. Tandor would have been overrun far sooner, and the demons would be wearing our skins if not for them.

When we reached the base of the mesa, Reverend Father Kilchii led us up a narrow road into a tunnel. From the tingle of magic against my skin, light balls were stationed on both sides every few steps so those with regular human sight could make their way without running into their companions. The roof was high enough to ride comfortably, but the pressure of the rock above us made it hard for me to breathe. Sweat broke out along every inch of my skin.

Are you all right? Luc murmured in my mind.

A bit of claustrophobia, I replied.

That's been a problem since you and Shi Hua collapsed the Death tunnel. His concern flowed through our link. *You didn't address that issue while you were at Child?*

Damn. I thought I'd hidden most of my fears in regard to enclosed spaces.

We had other priorities in my treatment, I bit back. Which was true. Especially since Ming Wei stopped me from striking my own squire Nathan. Or me possibly doing worse harm to him.

I'm sorry, my love. Luc withdrew, and I was thankful for the silence. It allowed me to focus on the calming exercises Mya had given me.

The tunnel curved to the left as it climbed, and I realized it was carved like the winding stairwell to the gaol like Orrin's Temple of Balance. Only on a much, much larger scale. We were probably circling the entire mesa.

I breathed a sigh of relief when we exited the tunnel onto the Diné version of Temple Street. The top of the mesa was noticeably cooler than the desert floor. That reason alone was enough to build up here. The only large stone buildings on the mesa were the Twelve Temples, the Guild Houses, and the Matriarch's Residence. However, the Guild Houses were smaller than I expected.

When I asked Gina about the difference in size compared to the Issuran Guild Houses, she smiled and said, "The Guild Houses are mainly used for storage during the summer and teaching during the winter months."

The Temples were oriented north and south as they were traditionally elsewhere in the world. They stood in the center of the mesa. Their architecture leaned toward a more simplistic style using the natural sandstone like Tandor had.

The Matriarch's Residence stood on the east side of the mesa. The three-story building was also built from sandstone, but it looked more like the descriptions I'd read of the Cliffdwellers' watch towers.

The Guild Houses were built in a similar style to the Matriarch's residence, but only consisted of two stories. They were arranged in a circular pattern around the mesa, equidistant from each of their neighbors.

Between the Guild Houses and the Temples, individual family dwellings seemed to grow straight from the ground. Dirt covered the homes, packed tight around the stones and wood that formed the frame. The design kept their hoogans warm in the winter and cool if the family stayed in Heart over the summer months. Nearly every single residence had a small garden surrounding it.

A child stood near the tunnel exit, his mouth agape at our appearance. Reverend Father Kilchii motioned him over. They spoke, and the boy dashed down the street between the Temples.

"He sent the boy to let the Diné Wildlings know they have an injured guest and to summon a healer," my warden murmured.

I turned to Gina. "If I didn't say so before, thank you for the additional cultural and language instruction. Is it selfish for me to ask you to stay in Orrin?"

"I hope you are jesting, m'lady," she murmured. "I've already accepted Chief Justice Elizabeth's request to be her new chief warden."

Part of me wasn't jesting at all, but I couldn't allow my own desires to stand in the way of Gina's advancement. "Don't worry, Warden. It's my inept way of apologizing for not appreciating what you bring to my Temple before now."

Her face and hands glowed crimson, and she nodded. "Thank you, Chief Justice."

We followed the Reverend Father to the Temple of Wildling where Sisquoc dismounted. The pain he tried to hide stabbed at my psyche. One of the Diné Wildling priests accompanied him up the three short steps into the building.

The Diné Thief priestess in front of me looked over her shoulder. "Worry not, Lady. Temples take care of our own no matter the nation," she said in heavily accented Issuran.

"Thank you, Sister," I replied in Diné. Despite her reassurance, I was still concerned about Sisquoc. As a Wildling, his ribs should be well on their way to healing even with him jouncing on a horse every night.

The portion of the column with Reverend Father Kilchii and his party and my contingent from Issura turned east between the Diné home Temples of Thief and Wildling. We headed straight to the Matriarch's Residence. Even though Luc and I were Temple, we were here as Queen Teodora's representatives. Out of habit since the night of the flash flood, I patted the lump in my right saddlebag that contained the sealed dispatches the Duke of Standora had delivered before sending us to Diné.

The lively conversations with my traveling companions kept me from questioning the contents over the last fortnight and two days. But what in Balance's Darkness would the queen entrust with me instead of a noble with far more diplomatic experience?

There was a large empty section where no hoogans stood halfway between the Temples and the Matriarch's Residence. The Reverend Father led us around that empty space. When I asked Gina about it, she smiled. "You'll see what it's for later tonight.

When we reached the pavilion before the Matriarch's Residence, Reverend Father Kilchii gave the signal for his people to dismount, so I did so as well. The rest of the Issuran party followed my lead.

My father turned the reins of his camel to one of his wardens and approached me. "If I may escort you inside, Chief Justice?" He held out his right hand, waiting for me to accept it rather than grabbing my left hand and wrapping it around his right elbow.

For once, someone didn't treat me as if I were a helpless blind woman. My eyes stung as I took his hand in mine.

Are you all right, Anthea? He whispered in my mind.

Yes, I— I cursed silently.

His lips twitched. Otherwise, he managed to keep a straight face, but his laughter rang in my head. *Your dislike of displaying emotion marks you as definitely one of mine.*

I bowed my head to hide my own expression of amusement. "One moment, Reverend Father. I have dispatches from Standora for various dignitaries here."

He nodded and released my fingers. I retrieved the small bag made of waterproofed leather from Nassa's saddlebag. Another tremor of unease rippled across my nerves, but I took my father's hand in mine again, and we headed toward the entrance of the Matriarch's residence.

Gina and Long Feather fell in step behind us, as did two of the Diné Conflict wardens. I didn't have to look behind me to know a majority of the Issuran party followed us while all of the peacekeepers, except Leyti, the remaining wardens, and Sister Migina remained outside with our horses.

The entrance into the Matriarch's Residence didn't have steps or anything that would indicate she held a more exalted status among her people. But then, the interior continental nations didn't deal with multiple identities like the coastal nations did. I found the difference fascinating. The entrance didn't have a door per se. The opening was tall and wide, and it was framed by two huge wool tapestries that were tied back. I wished I could see the designs woven into them.

The left one tells the story of our people traveling from the north, seeking warmth and food until Child led them here, Reverend Father Kilchii said silently. *The right one tells of our medicine woman of Balance called to Kemet. After we are finished with formal business, you can examine them through my eyes.*

Thank you. And I truly meant it. Both Gina and Dezba tried to teach me about my great-grandmother and father's people, but like me, they were more Issuran in thought and manner than Diné.

A central hall extended the entire length of the building. A tiny sliver of the rising scarlet sun framed the top edge of the eastern entrance. The interior was noticeably cooler, almost to the point I would have been chilled if I wore fewer clothes. The hallway was designed to capture mesa-top breezes and push the hotter air towards the opening in the roof three stories above us.

To our right, stone benches rose much like the gallery in my courtroom. A group from the Comanche Plains Nation sat there. I was surprised to recognize a couple of faces among the group.

However, I centered my attention on the one-step dais to my left. In the center was the Matriarch herself with an equal number of Diné elders on each side of her. The heads of the Temples, other than Reverend Father Kilchii, sat on the left side of the dais. The leaders of the Guilds sat on the right. They all sat on folding camp stools. The tableau seemed less ostentatious as such a gathering in Standora would appear, but far more solemn. There was a unity here Issura sorely needed.

The Matriarch herself wasn't as old as I expected. She was probably closer to Crown Princess Chiana's age of forty-one winters. We stopped before her and bowed.

"May I present Chief Justice Anthea of Orrin, who is here as a representative of Queen Teodora of Issura?" Reverend Father Kilchii said in Diné. His pleasant baritone echoed against the surrounding stone.

The Matriarch rose and smiled. "We welcome our friends from Issura, Chief Justice." Her Issuran was nearly free of accent.

"We come to serve," I said in Diné. "I have sayings from my Matriarch for you."

I could feel Gina and Long Feather wince behind me. I swear Diné was more difficult than Jing. By Balance, I had an easier time learning the Sea Peoples language. All I could do was keep my composure.

The Diné Matriarch chuckled. "Thank you for your effort, Chief Justice." She eyed Reverend Father Kilchii. "If you will bring these sayings to me."

I knew she was trying to soothe me, but her use of the wrong word didn't make me feel any better.

I handed the bag to the Reverend Father. He carried it on both of his palms and delivered it to the Matriarch. She opened it and examined the contents before passing dispatches to each of the other recipients.

The Reverend Father of Light glanced over his message before he nodded. "We grieve for the loss of your sister's child. My priests are at your disposal, Sister Zihna." My father silently translated for me.

"If you need additional aid, we are also at your disposal," the Reverend Mother of Love added. Behind me, Dezba repeated the words in Issuran to Zihna.

"Thank you for your assistance, Reverend Father, Reverend Mother," the Love priestess replied in Diné. Apparently, I wasn't the only one practicing during our trip here.

"Thank you," I said as well.

Once the clergy heads resumed their seats, the Diné chief of the Textile Guild rose next. She gestured to indicate the guild leaders. "We would like the opportunity to review the new proposed terms for expiring contracts and alterations to the current agreements."

"Of course, Chief Weaver." I bowed. "We will be here until the end of the Remembrance holiday, possibly a little longer."

"Given the weather oracles' prediction of heavy snow in the mountains this season, I suggest you hurry with your analysis," the Matriarch said. "Else we will be hosting the Issurans through the winter, and none of us will get what we want."

Most of the Elders and heads of the Temples chuckled. It appeared the chief weaver was doing her best not to make a face. However, a couple of her compatriots behind her didn't bother to hide their irritation at the Matriarch's comment.

The Matriarch cracked the seal on her rather large folded parchment. Three additional dispatches fell onto her lap. She examined the top one, and her good humor fled.

"Unless anyone has something they wish to address with our visitors?" The Matriarch stood, but she behaved as if she didn't expect anyone to question her. The clergy and guild chiefs shook their heads. "Very well then. We will meet to discuss the issues with Issura in three nights." She turned to the clergy. "Reverend Mother Hózhó, would you please join me and our sister from Issura for tea?"

The woman in Balance robes stood. "I would be honored, Matriarch."

The host Temples gathered the corresponding members of my party. Leyti looked at me for guidance.

"Go with Wardens Dezba and Mylon to the Temple of Balance," I said.

He nodded and followed the others out the west entrance.

One of the female Elders approached Lady Alessa. To my surprise, the duke's sister was quite fluent in the Diné language. Why hadn't she said anything about it for the last two weeks?

Alessa glided back to me. "We will be staying with Elder Doba. Our family has worked with her clan for decades."

"Very well." I nodded. "You know where to find me if you need anything."

Alessa grinned. "Of course, Chief Justice. You'll be wherever there is the most shouting and chaos."

I couldn't fault her opinion of me or my actions. I did have a tendency to find trouble. She returned to her friend. They were deep in conversation as they left.

When nearly everyone had cleared the chamber, the Matriarch strode over to me. "In order not to have any misunderstandings, we'll use your language, Chief Justice," she said in flawless Issuran before she cocked her head. "Anthea, we need to have a thorough discussion about why your own Reverend Mother wishes for my sister to slice through your pretty little neck."

Chapter 16

"I beg your pardon?" I could only stare at the leader of the Diné Nation as one of my worst fears came true.

Reverend Mother Hózhó snickered. "Nascha, I told you Alara is crazier than a Wixáritari Wildling priestess using peyōtl."

While I appreciated the Reverend Mother speaking in Issuran, it took me a moment to collect my spiraling emotions. "What is the basis of Reverend Mother Alara's charges?" I wish I could say I was surprised by my own Reverend Mother's actions, but weariness filled my soul. She had played too many games with me over the years.

The Matriarch waved one of the dispatches that had been in her packet. "This." She beckoned me to follow her. "I really need some tea in order to deal with more Issuran madness." She took Reverend Mother Hózhó's left hand and wrapped the priestess's fingers about the crook of her arm.

I glanced at my father, and then Luc. Both of them appeared as confused and irritated as I felt.

We and our wardens followed the Matriarch and the Diné Reverend Mother and their wardens. I gulped when we exited the eastern entrance. Circular benches surrounded unlit fire pits. Each set ringed the soil in a half circle with the doorway to the Residence at arch's center, but this wasn't a cooking area. It reminded me more of Sister Shi Hua's meditative gardens at both the Jing Embassy and the Orrin Temple of Light.

The most amazing thing was the vista. The view from the edge of the mesa seemed like I stood on a cloud. Past the yellow fields, orange desert spread out to the horizon. The thin green threads of irrigation canals spread out from the river far below us.

As much as I wanted to indulge in the scenery the overlook provided, I needed to deal with the latest problem dumped on me. I turned to face the others.

"Wardens, go sit over there," The Matriarch snapped in Diné as she glared at our guards and waved the dispatches in her hand in the direction of the benches on the opposite end of the arch. "The Reverend Father and I have no plans to throw each other off the cliff today."

The Diné wardens chuckled at her words, and Gina translated for the Issuran Light wardens. However, both Gina and Long Feather eyed me with a measure of concern. I dipped my head, and they followed Luc's wardens to the benches the Matriarch had indicated.

The Matriarch led Reverend Mother Hózhó to the northern-most bench before she sat next to the priestess and handed her one of the dispatches.

She turned her glare on me and switched back to Issuran. "Come over and sit down, Anthea. I won't bite you. I save that for Kilchii." She leered at my father.

He grinned in return and gestured for me and Luc to take seats. "Ignore Nascha, Anthea. She's only insufferable with family."

"Family?" I froze.

"From my understanding, you have more family here in Diné than you do in Issura," Reverend Mother Hózhó said. "We're happy Kilchii finally met you despite the circumstances in Tandor. I was quite tickled to hear my cousin was a Balance seat in Issura."

"Um…I…well—" I couldn't gather my thoughts at this revelation.

It left me grasping for words as well as the breath with which to say them.

"I apologize, Matriarch. I don't know what's wrong with her." Luc nudged me with his elbow. "When we were on circuit, I couldn't get her to shut up for the last nine years."

The Diné leaders laughed at his jibe. I shook my head and claimed the free place next to Reverend Mother Hózhó.

"I apologize, Reverend Mother," I said. "I've learned more about my personal family in the last nine months than I knew in my previous thirty winters." I wanted to ask how we were related, but such a personal question was incredibly rude in the midst of a diplomatic meeting.

"Family is family no matter what, my dear." She pushed back her hood and smiled in my direction. "And I trust Kilchii's opinion of you more than whatever my counterpart says." She waved the dispatch again. "I could accidentally lose it to the wind."

"No, don't do that," I said sharply. Her humor abruptly disappeared, and I realized I'd overstepped propriety.

"I apologize again, Reverend Mother, for my lack of etiquette." I folded my hands and tried to appear contrite to the Matriarch and Reverend Father Kilchii. "Please do as you will with the dispatch. However, I do wish to know the charges against me. Even if you believe they are inconsequential, I need to know what I'm facing when I return to Orrin."

She ran her fingers over the seal. "It's unbroken, Nascha. How do you know Alara wants to behead the girl?"

"Within a packet addressed to me was your dispatch from Alara, a letter from Teodora to me mentioning her concern over Alara possibly using us to dispose of Anthea—" The Matriarch held out the third letter to me. "—and a letter from Reverend Father Gray Shadow of Thief for Anthea."

I blinked as I tried to process what the Matriarch said. "By the Twelve, why—" I took the parchment from her and looked at Luc sitting on my right.

He shrugged. "High Brother Talbert mentioned his Reverend Father had a vested interest in keeping you alive."

"But why—"

"We need to know what all three letters say, Anthea, in order to suss out the truth," my father said from his seat next to the Matriarch.

Luc placed his hand on my spine. His warm magic calmed me. I sucked in a deep breath. My fingers confirmed the wax was stamped with the seal of Reverend Father Gray Shadow. However, the wax contained a subtle spell.

Do you sense this? I asked silently while projecting the sensation to Luc.

No. He frowned, and I could perceive him checking the seal. *Does it feel like demon magic?*

I shook my head.

Thief magic tuned to you personally? he asked.

I closed my eyes and carefully prodded the spell. It reacted to me, like a puppy's licks or a kitten's purr. *It would appear so.*

Active light magic tingled across my skin. "I have a ward prepped," Luc murmured. "Reverend Father, you and the ladies might wish to step away."

"What is it?" Reverend Mother Hózhó asked.

"A spell within the wax keyed to me personally." I opened my eyes and sighed. "It wouldn't be the first time the renegades, the Assassins Guild, or the demons laid a trap for me. Maybe you should go inside the Residence."

A buzzing sounded inside my mind as the three Diné discussed the matter silently. Reverend Father Kilchii regarded me, and the harsh vibration of Conflict magic made the small hairs all over my body stand on end.

"I can ward Nascha, Hózhó, and myself," he said. "Should we send the wardens inside for their protection?"

"No," I answered. "The spell is keyed to me so the effects shouldn't spread beyond this immediate fire pit circle." I looked at Luc. "Ready?"

"Yes."

I held the dispatch away from my body, took a deep breath, and broke the seal.

Nothing happened.

Or rather, nothing magical happened. The spell caressed my psyche, and its energy dispersed. Probably to let Reverend Father Gray Shadow know I had received his message. It was an interesting bit of magic, similar to a reverse tracking spell.

"Well, that was rather anticlimactic," the Matriarch said sourly.

"It's better than finding a priestess's body in a wine barrel," I replied dryly.

"Or getting your foot chopped off," Luc added.

"Demons using a peacekeeper and his family to hatch their eggs," I said.

"Finding the Love head of household face down in the high sister's bath." Luc eyed me.

"Losing over half of the seats of Tandor and Orrin," I said softly.

"Gerd murdering my unborn son." Luc choked on the words, and a wave of grief flowed from him.

The Diné stared at us in shock and horror.

Finally, Reverend Mother Hózhó said, "This has not been a year blessed by the Twelve for you two, has it?"

"Not when the only guidance I've received from Balance was when she told me to jump off a cliff." I laughed hysterically. The Matriarch and Reverend Mother Hózhó continued to stare at me as if I'd lost my mind. However, both Luc and Reverend Father Kilchii chuckled.

"You'll get used to Anthea's black sense of humor," Father said.

"Else you will join the renegades because they find her equally annoying," Luc added.

Sometimes, I wondered how close to the truth Luc's statement was.

Chapter 17

I brushed my fingers over the second parchment within the piece sealed with wax. The letter had been stamped using the Balance code of raised marks. Reverend Father Gray Shadow wasn't a fool. He made sure I could read his letter and concealed the coded message within another letter.

"Is there anything on this piece?" I handed the outer parchment to Luc.

He cleared his throat. "To Chief Justice Anthea of Orrin, Your recent recommendation of Sister Cedar Grove to a seat has been received. High Brother Talbert has been equally glowing in his praise of her. However, I believe it's in the best interest of Issura that I do not cause more chaos by reassigning members of my order given the recent events in both the cities of Tandor and Orrin. That does not mean the sister will not be considered for a seat in the near future. May the Twelve watch over you. Reverend Father Gray Shadow, blah, blah, blah."

"'Blah, blah, blah'?" Reverend Father Kilchii frowned. "Is that how you refer to your superiors, High Brother?"

"The titles and flowery words at the end are irrelevant to Reverend Father Gray Shadow, sir," I said as I unfolded the second parchment. "And to me as well. High Brother Talbert made a point of sending two of his clergy with us on our trip. Thief has been doing their best to watch my back since the chaos started in Orrin at midwinter. The cover

95

letter is Reverend Father Gray Shadow's method of apologizing for not doing more."

"It's sad you think more like Thief than Balance," Reverend Father Kilchii said.

"Yes, sir, it is," I replied before I read the second letter. The silence of the Diné while I digested the message made me appreciate that part of my heritage. But the contents of Gray Shadow's letter chilled my blood.

Thankfully, members of the Matriarch's household staff brought steaming pots of teas and plates of hot sweet corn cakes and skewers of mutton. My stomach growled at the delicious smells, and I wondered if they would taste similar to the dishes Gina and Dezba made on the Rest Days when they cooked the Balance staff's dinner. The Matriarch staff's appearance gave me a chance to reread the stamped letter. As much as I wished, the contents had not changed. The news was distressing, probably more so to Thief, but there wasn't a damn thing I could do from here.

"How can you feel hunger, rage, and sorrow at the same time, Anthea?" Reverend Mother Hózhó asked once the staff had retreated.

"That's her normal state, Reverend Mother," Luc answered. "It's particularly embarrassing when we are investigating the scene of a murder, and her stomach starts growling."

"If the populace would wait until after I've broken my fast before getting themselves killed or their bodies discovered, it would be much better for everyone involved," I bit out before I turned to the Reverend Mother. "Often I cannot finish my first cup of tea in the morning before I'm summoned lately."

The Matriarch wore an appalled expression. "You have that many homicides in the Duchy of Orrin?"

"Oh, no, not the duchy. This is only the city of Orrin." I took a sip from my cup. The tea wasn't the Jing black I favored, but it was quite delicious.

"Certainly your own Reverend Mother of Balance would send you assistance—" Reverend Father Kilchii started.

"Not if Alara wants the girl out of the way," Reverend Mother Hózhó growled. "So where the Assassins Guild and the demons failed, now she wants us to perform the task. Kilchii says you can see demons through their shapeshifting and illusions."

"Up to a point, m'lady." I glanced at my father. "I cannot perceive them if the demons are wearing human skins."

The Matriarch made a hissing sound. "We do not speak of such things, child."

"With all due respect, Matriarch, not speaking of certain things is why we're in trouble now," I said as gracefully as I could manage. "And I'm speaking of true demons, our foes, not the others your people refer to skinwalkers."

"What do you mean?" Reverend Mother Hózhó asked.

"We should not be speaking of this," the Matriarch spat.

"Knowledge is our best weapon, Nascha," Reverend Father Kilchii said. "And we've lost much over the last century. There's no human left who remembers the last demon incursion, and we nearly lost a chunk of our clergy because of the things we've forgotten. Why do you think I've been spending so much time in Knowledge?"

The Matriarch snorted. "I thought it was the attractive Sister Lizard drawing your attention."

"Sister Lizard was instrumental in helping us destroy the demon army, Matriarch," I said. "I would be relying on her research skills if I were in the Reverend Father's place."

"He may be your birth father, Anthea, but you don't know him," she said archly.

"Being a product of the Spring Rituals, I shouldn't know him at all, Matriarch." I gave her a wry smile. "But he has been far more honorable in the short time I've known him than my birth mother was her entire life."

"One should not speak of their parents thusly either," the Matriarch snapped.

"You mean like how my birth mother Gerd became a true skinwalker and slaughtered High Brother Luc's unborn child in an attempt to fuel a spell that would destroy Orrin?" I said.

The Matriarch gaped at me, but Reverend Mother Hózhó didn't look a bit surprised.

"So she didn't head east to get out of Issura as Alara guessed?" the head of Balance murmured.

"No, Reverend Mother," I replied. "In the space between Gerd's arrest and her return to Orrin, she began practicing demon magic." A shudder ran through me at the memory of the awful day she abducted me and stabbed Claudia. "I have to ask, Reverend Mother Hózhó. Did you receive anything official from Reverend Mother Alara about Gerd's escape from the home Temple in Balance?"

The Diné priestess's face crinkled. "No. That was going to be my next question for you. What did she tell you about the escape?"

"Nothing, m'lady. Absolutely nothing." A sip of tea soothed my dry mouth. "I found out about it through High Sister Dragonfly of Love. I've lost track of how many queries I've sent to my home Temple about the breakout, but my clerks could count them if you wish. However, I have received no answer from anyone at the home Temple in Standora. I'm surprised she said anything to you at all about the escape."

"In this letter—" Reverend Mother Hózhó held up the stamped parchment she received. "—Alara says you are in possession of a demon grimoire."

"What in Conflict does she expect Anthea to say?" Reverend Father Kilchii snapped. "If she really did have an illegal grimoire, why would she tell us the truth?"

"Did Reverend Mother Alara tell you the part where Anthea originally confiscated that particular grimoire and turned it over to the Reverend Mother for destruction?" Luc wore a wolfish smile similar to the one High Brother Jax wore when the machinations of non-Wildling humans amused him. "That she failed to destroy the grimoire? Or that Gerd stole the grimoire back during her escape?"

"She left those parts out," Reverend Mother Hózhó said dryly. "Please tell me you've destroy the cursed thing."

"Yes, Reverend Mother." Luc's voice was firm and confident. "Sister Claudia and I burned it to ash, and then Justice Yanaba aged the ashes until they were nothing but a few bits of dust. The other ten seats witnessed the destruction, along with Chief Justice Elizabeth, formerly of Tandor, acting as the official Balance representative."

"Where were you during the grimoire's destruction, Anthea?" The Matriarch whispered the question as if she feared the answer.

"In a cell in the Temple of Child," I replied. "The demons tried to use the grimoire to control me. If it weren't for Justice Yanaba's squire Ming Wei, they would have driven me mad."

Luc snorted.

I chuckled. "Well, madder than I am already. Or they would have seduced me into using the grimoire." A shiver ran through me despite the heat of the day. My experience with that damned book had been a close thing indeed.

"Read this." Reverend Mother Hózhó held out the stamped parchment Reverend Mother Alara had sent to her. She didn't have to allow me to review the dispatch. A bit of me was grateful she took my testimony seriously as I accepted the letter.

My fingertips danced over the raised symbols, my anger growing with each word.

"What is it?" Luc murmured.

It was poor form to criticize the leader of one's Temple in front of clergy from another order, much less another nation, but my Reverend Mother was the one who dragged the Diné into our internal problems.

"She told Reverend Mother Hózhó just enough of the truth to make me look guilty," I bit out.

"Why would she do such a thing?" the Matriarch said.

Luc and I looked at each other. I wasn't sure if her question was rhetorical, but I answered anyway.

"She doesn't know the grimoire has been destroyed," I murmured. "Or she thinks the demons have gained control of me, and it's a test to see if I've corrupted you and the other Diné leaders, both Temple and civilian, yet."

Reverend Mother Hózhó made a sound deep in her chest. "So she's either covering her arse, or she's a renegade."

"Then there's only one thing you can do, Anthea." Reverend Father scowled at me, but I didn't think his fury was aimed at me. "Truthspell us."

Chapter 18

I could only stare at my father. "Do you truly comprehend what you are saying?"

"Wait a moment!" The Matriarch's attention frantically flipped from him to Reverend Mother Hózhó and back. "I don't agree to foreign clergy placing any spell on me, much less a truthspell, even if she is family."

"It's the only way for our guests to be sure of us," Reverend Father Kilchii stated. "They didn't have to say a word about their queendom's problems."

"You don't know her any more than she knows you," the Matriarch protested. "Sometimes, the truth can be someone's greatest weapon."

"Let's assume Alara is just an idiot and not a renegade," Reverend Mother Hózhó said. "She is betraying our entire order by omitting pertinent information in her letter about one of our justices. We aren't ordinary priestesses. If someone in Balance makes a mistake in our duties, civilians suffer. It doesn't matter if it's loss of life, loss of property, or worst of all, loss of faith that we will uphold the highest standards of ethics and morals. Furthermore, Alara has failed Anthea by not even doing her the courtesy of admitting Gerd escaped from Alara's custody."

"By Alara not giving Orrin proper warning, she allowed Gerd to kill Luc and Claudia's unborn child," Reverend Father Kilchii added. "She's guilty of negligent homicide by her omission, if nothing else."

101

"Plus Alara's failures are the reason their Sister Zihna had to petition our Temple of Light for permission to conceive with one of them." Reverend Mother Hózhó scowled. "Anthea, what did Gray Shadow say in his letter to you?"

"He reiterated the same information our queen sent to your Matriarch, concerning the letter Reverend Mother Alara sent to you." I hesitated a moment. "I would like to privately discuss the remaining issues he addressed with my fellow seats before revealing anything more. Thief has done it's best to watch mine and High Brother Luc's backs against the renegades, the Assassins Guild, and the demons. I do not wish to accidentally betray them by saying the wrong thing to the wrong person."

The Matriarch smiled at me. "I can see why you've earned the trust of both Kilchii and Teodora. However, I will not blindly submit to a truthspell, young lady."

"You'd be under a truthspell for any trade agreements we'd make with Issura." Reverend Father Kilchii grinned. "What are you really afraid of, Nascha?"

Her mouth pressed into a moue, but I wasn't sure of the emotion behind it. For someone who wasn't Temple, her emotions were tightly shielded. But then I noticed the same thing with our Crown Princess Chiara. It was a useful talent to have when one wasn't sure of the intentions of foreign dignitaries.

"She's probably worried to discover the mothers of your other children were better in bed than she was," Reverend Mother Hózhó said dryly.

It was all I could do to keep my mouth shut at the Diné priestess's jab. Luc managed to turn his bark of surprise and humor into a coughing fit. On the other hand, Reverend Father Kilchii laughed outright as the Matriarch's skin shifted from yellow-orange to red-orange.

Sometimes, my odd sight offered me more information about a person's emotion than my mental talents could.

The Matriarch quelled her embarrassment and ignored the Reverend Mother. "Once you and your party have a chance to rest and discuss the surprises your own people have laid upon us, we will talk more, Chief Justice."

Both Luc and I stood and bowed. "Thank you for your patience in this matter, Matriarch," I said.

Reverend Mother Hózhó rose as well. "Kilchii and I will escort you back to the Temples." She held out her left hand in my general direction.

Suspicion immediately swept through me. I couldn't deny the courtesy of her request without our hosts taking offense, but I didn't like to have my sword arm encumbered. In the end, etiquette won. I took her fingers and wrapped them about the crook of my right arm.

When we took our leave from the Matriarch's Residence, none of our wardens appeared happy that they couldn't separate the four of us. But the situation turned out to my benefit.

"I hope Nascha didn't offend you too much," Reverend Mother Hózhó murmured. "My sister has a bad habit of letting her personal feelings for Kilchii get in the way of her diplomatic duties."

I blinked. The priestess had used the Diné word for blood relation, instead of the variety of other words that all translated into "sister" in Issuran.

"You weren't jesting about us being related," I said.

"By the Twelve, no!" She shook her head. "I would never joke about something like that. My great-aunt Tibah was your great-grandmother. It nearly broke her heart to leave Thalia in Issura, but it was the law. What could she do?"

"Did she keep in touch with Thalia?" I asked.

"No, it simply wasn't allowed back then." Reverend Mother Hózhó reached over and patted my right arm with her right hand. "You have to remember everyone still expected a demon attack at any time when your grandmother was born."

"So we're not related through my father?" I asked.

The Reverend Mother laughed long and loud. Several of the Diné wardens snickered or coughed.

"Hey!" Kilchii protested behind us.

"You've met Kilchii and Nascha's son Brother Bumblebee," the Reverend Mother stated.

"Bumblebee . . . is my brother?" My mind tried to wrap itself around the new knowledge. After being alone for so long, discovering I had a sibling was . . . fantastic and frightening at the same time.

"You have three siblings, Anthea," Kilchii volunteered behind me.

"That we know of," Reverend Mother Hózhó said dryly. More snickers came from the wardens behind us.

She leaned closer to me, released my elbow, and clasped my hand in hers. *Nascha wanted him to leave the order so they could wed. She took his refusal as a sign he found her wanting when he knew that civilian life was not for him.*

I found myself really liking Hózhó. Part of me wished she was Issura's Reverend Mother of Balance. But it was foolish to desire such things. We each had the thread of life Balance gave us. It wasn't wise to long for things I couldn't have.

It had taken more than one incident before I truly learned that lesson.

We stopped in the space between the Temples of Balance and Light. I was exhausted. However, by the time we adjusted to being awake during the daylight hours again, it would be time for us to return across the desert to Issura.

We thanked the Reverend Father for his escort. He'd taken a couple of steps away before I called out, "Reverend Father?"

"Yes, Chief Justice?" As usual, he seemed highly amused by me formally addressing him. Maybe Shi Hua's Reverend Father of Conflict could take some lessons from Kilchii, assuming Reverend Father Chen was still alive. He'd disappeared into the Gobi Desert on the other side of the world roughly eight months ago, chasing after more of the demon eggs that had been laid in our plane of existence.

"Do the Diné Temples have tunnel systems like those in Issura?"

His attention flicked to Luc before he shook his head. "The old tribes believed the mesas were secured enough by their height, and it's easy enough to defend the single tunnel to the top or even collapse it if we have to."

I inclined my head. "That knowledge is actually very reassuring."

"Good dreams, Anthea." He headed for the Temple of Conflict, his retinue trailing along behind him.

I hoped for once this year I would indeed have them.

Chapter 19

Sialealea, the Diné Balance staff member assigned to us, woke Gina, Dezba, and me shortly before the Temple bells rang First Evening. A kerfluffle with the Balance head of household had erupted over the two wardens sleeping in the room I was assigned. As I told Reverend Mother Hózhó, my wardens' precautions had more to do with the Assassins Guild having a price on my head than any insult or aspersion to the Diné Nation. In turn, the Reverend Mother pointed out to her head of household that my death through her negligence meant her own neck would be introduced to the sharp edge of the Reverend Mother's sword.

After a proper trial of course.

The Balance head of household acceded to Reverend Mother Hózhó's logic and had extra beds placed in the room for my wardens. I wasn't sure if the head of household assigned Sialealea to us out of some wrongdoing on her part, because she was the youngest member of the staff, or because she didn't know a single word of Issuran. In the end, it didn't matter. The girl gave me a chance to practice my skills with the Diné language.

Since water was such a scarce resource in Diné, I still could not have a proper bath. Instead, Sialealea used oil and skin scrapers to clean my body as I lay on a long wooden table in what would have been the bathing room of the guest quarters in Issura. I heard her hiss of horror when I rolled over on the table, and she saw the scars on my back.

"The lashes were her punishment for defying Balance and giving herself sight," Gina said in Diné. "It's best not to speak of it."

"Sh-she can see?" Sialealea blurted.

I turned on my side to face the girl. "She can hear, too."

"I beg your forgiveness, Lady Justice." Sialealea looked everywhere but directly at me.

"Child, you offer me not wrong," I said. Gina leaned against the wall, and from her smirk, I'd gotten some words or inflection wrong again. At least, she didn't correct me in front of the girl and undermine my authority. "Do your task, thank you."

Frustration filled me as Gina's smirk turned into a full grin.

"I mean you have offered me no insult," I said to Sialealea before I switched to Issuran and addressed Gina. "You know I'm useless upon waking without my Jing tea."

"That's why Warden Mylon is fetching you some hot water, m'lady."

I laid on my stomach once again, and Sialealea started on the back of my right leg. I muttered, "The water is useless without the leaves, Warden."

"That's the reason every Temple member is carrying a small pack of Jing black in their stores," Gina retorted.

I jerked up on my elbows and glared at her. "You mean everyone had Jing tea with them, and no one said a word to me?"

My warden shrugged. "You weren't acting particularly yourself during our ride here, so we saved it for emergencies like now."

"You mean surly upon waking?"

"I was trying not to say that, m'lady," Gina responded.

I lay my head back down and decided to keep my silence until Mylon returned with the hot water. At that moment, I truly realized how much I was going to miss Gina when she left with Elizabeth next spring.

While we were asleep, a Cliff Dwellers delegation arrived at Heart. The Diné turned our visits into a major celebration. And the location for the feasting and dancing was the large open area I'd noted when we arrived.

Thankfully, the manners of the Diné, the Cliff Dwellers, and the Plains Nations people precluded anyone from commenting on my eyes. However, I did catch occasional furtive looks and warding signs in my peripheral vision.

While Reverend Mother Hózhó and the other Diné justices were seated on benches at the edge of the circle, Dezba and I circulated among the crowd. There were quite a few folks involved in the siege of Tandor present, and it was good make our reacquaintance.

When my stomach growled loud enough it could be heard over the crowd, Dezba guided me to one of the food tables. I'd finished my sweet corn cakes when someone called out, "Chief Justice Anthea?"

At the question in a familiar voice that didn't have a Diné accent, I turned to my right. A glee overtook me that had nothing to do with my diplomatic mission.

"High Brother Pecos!" I enveloped the Comanche Conflict priest in a hug. The bison fur that wrapped his braids tickled my cheek. We'd spent many a night together on the watchtowers of Tandor during the demon siege last spring. "It's so good to see you again!"

He laughed and hugged me back. "I don't remember you being this physically demonstrative in Tandor."

"I think that had more to do with my own terrible body odor." I leaned back and grinned at him. "I couldn't stand the smell of myself so I kept my distance from everyone."

He chuckled. "We all felt that way." A mischievous expression crossed his face and he switched to his own language. "How much Comanche do you remember?"

"Absolutely nothing," I responded in kind.

His laughter died, and he hesitated a moment before he said in Issuran, "May I speak to you privately for a moment?"

"Of course," I said.

Dezba laid her hand on the hilt of her knife. "I'll be nearby, m'lady." The look she gave Pecos could have incinerated a demon.

"I vow to Conflict I mean no harm to the chief justice," Pecos replied with a bow.

"Warden Tyra can—" It was the first time I'd said her name since the week we'd returned to Orrin. The loss struck me like a blow to the gut. She couldn't vouch for Pecos's character.

"We share your grief," he said softly. "I wouldn't dishonor such a great warrior by injuring her charge."

"Nor would I by allowing harm to the chief justice when my friend worked so hard to keep her alive." Dezba stepped closer to Pecos. "I will still remain within hearing distance."

"Stop it, you two," I snapped. "We are guests, and this is a celebration. Whatever you need to say to me, Brother, on my honor, I swear to my warden's silence."

"I have a delivery for Ambassador Quan from my Reverend Father," Pecos said. "However, I cannot continue to Issura with it without questions being asked. May I impose on you to deliver it to him?"

I cocked an eyebrow. "Brother, you know it's bad manners to conduct business during a social function."

"Unfortunately, I fear I will not have another chance to speak privately to you, Chief Justice," he murmured.

"Very well, I'd be honored to assist both of you." I inclined my head. "I assume it is ingredients for the recipe he shared with you for your Reverend Father."

"Yes, and the Reverend Father was quite pleased with the baking results."

"Excellent." I smiled. "Deliver it to Balance tomorrow. Will Warden Dezba be an acceptable substitute if I'm not there?" From the corner of my eye, I saw her face shift into an unpleasant expression.

"Most acceptable," Pecos said. "Are you staying until the holiday?" He leaned closer. "Or do you believe it's bad luck to travel during the Day of Death like the Diné?"

"It's not about ill luck. Death should be honored appropriately," I murmured. "Just like any other member of the Twelve."

"I did not mean insult, Chief Justice." Pecos shook his head. "It's just—" He heaved a sigh. "The Diné Reverend Father of Conflict is the only one taking the renegades and their adaptation of demon magic seriously. Any Diné clergy who did not participate in the Battle of Tandor and all their civilians treat the subject as taboo."

"I've noticed," I said dryly. "But believe me when I say you cannot force a blind person to see."

He cocked his head, not sure whether to be appalled or humored by my statement. From his half-hearted chuckle, he decided on the latter. "Point taken, Chief Justice."

Now that everyone had a chance to eat, the low cadence of drums vibrated through the soil. People cleared the area in the middle.

When rattles were added, the Matriarch and another man moved to stand on opposite sides of the space. The cadence of the drums picked up and they began dancing around the circle to the song the observers chanted. After the pair completed one full circuit, others joined in, the women behind the Matriarch and the men behind her partner. Each dancer clasped the right shoulder of the person in front of them with their right hand.

Pecos took two steps toward the circle before he looked over his shoulder at us. "Are you two joining?"

"You don't want me dancing." I shook my head. "I'd break everyone's toes."

"No, thank you," Dezba murmured.

"Who's the man leading the dance with the Matriarch?" I whispered to Dezba once Pecos was in the circle.

"Her eldest brother Niyol," she replied. She glanced around us before she added, "From what I learned at their Temple of Balance, she's never married. She wanted Reverend Father Kilchii to leave the order of Conflict so they could wed, but he refused. Supposedly, when she learned about Duke White Eagle and Crown Princes Chiara, she flew into such a rage, her family feared she would injure herself."

"The clan elders still elected her as matriarch after that?" I asked.

Dezba shrugged. "Brother Bumblebee was born after that. Prior to their relationship, all of your father's other children were products of the Spring Rituals."

"Thank you for the reminder," I said dryly.

"My observation wasn't meant to insult you, m'lady," Dezba replied. "It's just—" She twitched, and her skin darkened to a red-orange.

"You have my permission to speak freely, Dezba," I said. "If this will affect our mission, I need to know."

"I was surprised High Brother Pecos didn't address your relationship." She frowned.

"What relationship is that?" I asked.

"He's your half-brother, too."

"Oh." I turned to watch him dance. The two lines had joined together, alternating dancers, into one long string. Somehow, learning my connection with Pecos made sense. "He may not know. Or he does, and he didn't know if I knew." I looked at Dezba again. "Is that why you were making faces behind his back?"

She lifted her chin. "I don't wish to see your equilibrium damaged. You've had so much thrown at you over the last year. I personally don't wish to see you hurt any more than you have been."

It finally struck me what she was truly worried about. "Dezba, none of you have failed me. My issues existed long before I was made the seat of Balance in Orrin. If anything, I've failed all of you, especially Aglaia and Tyra."

"They performed their duties to the fullest extent," Dezba said.

"They did, but it was my choices that led to their deaths." I shook my head. "Not theirs—"

A shrill scream echoed through the night. The percussionists and dancers came to a jagged halt. The scream repeated and was joined by more shouts and cries from the direction of the Matriarch's Residence.

Dezba and I raced for the building, dodging people milling about and asking each other foolish questions. Other wardens and clergy ran toward the Matriarch's residence as well. I pushed my way past the clustered, silent crowd at the entrance.

Above us, a rope creaked. It swayed from the weight of the corpse hanging from it.

Chapter 20

"Can we have one month without someone being murdered?" I growled at the Issuran clergy gathered in one of the Balance reception rooms. "Just one blasted month!"

"Are you upset about the death or that Reverend Mother Hózhó rejected your offer of assistance?" Luc asked.

"Both, actually." I shrugged. "I know it's not my jurisdiction, but we have far too much experience in these kind of matters."

"Which is exactly why we're sitting in Balance," Sister Migina slumped in her chair. "We're not Diné, so of course we're primary suspects."

"If the Reverend Mother thought we were involved, we'd be in their gaol and chained with spell-threaded manacles," Sister Claudia said. "Not to mention, we were all at the festivities tonight with our wardens nearby."

"Unfortunately, that's why the wardens and peacekeepers who accompanied us were placed in a different Temple." High Brother Ben rubbed his temples.

"Sister Zihna wasn't there," Brother Piru said softly.

Claudia reached over and smacked the back of the Conflict priest's head while Zihna glared at him.

"Ow!" Piru rubbed the spot Claudia had struck.

"She's been at Love since we arrived, idiot," Claudia snapped.

"And in the middle of mating when I was dragged over here," Zihna added.

"You could have said that instead of hitting me," he protested.

"Brother Sisquoc wasn't there either," Migina bit out. "Is he guilty, too?"

I slapped the tabletop for attention. "Everybody needs to stop hitting everyone and accusing each other. There's no sense doing the demons work for them."

"Have you seen . . ." Luc's worry prickled against my psyche.

I shook my head. "No, but it would be very easy to stay out of my sight here in Heart." I didn't want to add to his concerns, but it needed to be addressed. "And I can't see demons dressed in human skins."

"I haven't smelled any demons either," Sister Farrah murmured. "This could be the work of renegades or the Assassins Guild."

"Why would they hang someone?" Ben asked. "I thought they preferred poison or a knife."

"They'd hang someone and use the death energy to cast a demon spell." Luc stared at me. "They don't necessarily have to be a demon or a skinwalker to do that."

"We don't even know who died tonight," I pointed out. "There's a number of reasons why a human might have done this."

"So we're going to avoid the possibility it might be suicide?" Zihna asked.

"We're not." I rose and started to pace the little room. "But even if the Temple of Child missed the signs in the deceased, someone else would have noticed a change in behavior. Besides, if someone's in that much emotional pain they want to end their life, they would pick somewhere private for such an obvious action."

"You sound like your talking from experience," Ben said.

I shrugged. "If I wanted to die as much as you all think, I would have let one of the Assassins Guild attempts succeed. But consider this.

Why hang yourself when there's such a cultural taboo worldwide, not just here on the Northern Long Continent? Furthermore, why would you do it in possibly the most public place in Heart? The Matriarch's Residence is the center of the civilian government."

"Perhaps I wanted to make a statement," Luc offered. "Especially with dignitaries from Issura and the Plains Nations here for trade negotiations."

"Or are we here for more than trade negotiations?" Claudia leaned her elbows on the pine tabletop. "Is there some task the queen placed on you two? The Duke of Standora doesn't come to Orrin twice in one year for no reason."

Luc and I looked at each other for a long moment.

"They need to know," he said softly.

I sighed. "Let me ward the room first."

Anxiety sprouted among our fellow clergy at my words. It couldn't be helped. Plus, I told the Matriarch and Reverend Mother Hózhó I'd be more forthcoming once I'd discussed Reverend Father Gray Shadow's letter with the Issuran clergy.

Once I'd circled the room and my wards were in place, everyone looked expectantly at me as I took my seat again.

"This cannot go beyond these walls. All of your lives depend on it," I started. "There was a special packet from the queen. In it were three letters: one from Reverend Mother Alara to Reverend Mother Hózhó, one from Queen Teodora to the Matriarch, and one from Reverend Father Gray Shadow to me."

Sister Malila and Brother Teluhci of Thief looked at each other with confused expressions before Teluhci turned to me and said, "Why in the names of the Twelve would he do that?"

"Because neither he nor Queen Teodora trust the couriers right now," Luc said. "The letter to Reverend Mother Hózhó insinuates

Chief Justice Anthea has in her possession a demon grimoire and is using it."

The room erupted into protests. Loud protests. I was rather glad I'd warded the room.

"Calm down, everyone," Ben shouted over the brothers and sisters. "Let the Chief Justice finish."

Claudia jumped to her feet and pounded on the table. "But Luc and I destroyed the blasted thing!"

"That's not letting me finish, Sister," I said dryly.

The Love priestess struggled to pull herself together while Zihna tugged on Claudia's arm. She finally resumed her seat. "My apologies, Chief Justice."

"None of the Orrin seats have told their superiors about the grimoire I confiscated a second time from Gerd because we're trying to flush out who knew about it," I said.

Sister Malila muttered several obscenities. Everyone else's eyes widened as they put the facts together. Sister Nina of Vintner shook her head in denial.

"No, a Reverend Mother or Father couldn't possibly—"

"We don't know for sure who actually stamped the letter allegedly from Reverend Mother Alara," Luc said.

"Queen Teodora was obviously worried about what may be in the letter from Balance," I said. "She wrote a letter to the Diné Matriarch to question any correspondence from Balance. The letter from Reverend Father Gray Shadow was to warn me of the same."

"It's not like a home Temple to bypass the local seat," Ben said. "Do we need to worry about Talbert?" Nearly everyone's attention focused on the two Thief clergy. I had to give the pair credit. Neither Malila nor Teluhci flinched from the others' regard.

"No, it's not, but these are unusual times." I relaxed a little now that my fellows were thinking, not yelling. "Reverend Father Gray Shadow has probably already informed High Brother Talbert of all the issues with the home Temple of Balance."

"What other issues?" Brother Piru asked.

I sucked in a deep breath. "The watcher Thief placed in Balance has disappeared, and the queen's distance speaker was poisoned shortly before we left Orrin."

Everyone, including Luc stared at me with stunned expressions.

"The Reverend Father mentioned those in the letter?" Luc asked.

I nodded.

"I don't quite understand why he told you and not us or even High Brother Talbert," Teluhci said.

"Your Temple has been watching my back for the last year and a half." I smiled gently at the younger priest. "Matters have escalated to the point in Issura where someone is contriving to get the Diné Temple of Balance to kill me since the Assassins Guild has repeatedly failed."

"And you're a key target because you can see demons," Migina murmured.

"Yes."

"How did the Matriarch and Reverend Mother Hózhó take the alleged request from Reverend Mother Alara?" Ben asked.

Luc chuckled. "With a great deal of annoyance toward Reverend Mother Alara. Reverend Father Kilchii let it slip they've been in regular contact with Standora. The crown doesn't want it known they have a second distance speaker."

"The queen and the crown princess are seeing more problems within Standora, aren't they?" Claudia said.

I smiled at her. "Luc and I have a feeling the reason we were sent to Diné was so the queen, the crown princess, and Reverend Father Gray Shadow could do their own flushing at home."

"Whoever the renegade spy is within Balance, they are highly placed." Milila drummed her fingertips against the tabletop.

"That's assuming it's not the Reverend Mother herself," Zihna mused.

From everyone's expressions, none of us liked that possibility. But if Reverend Mother Alara was attempting to manipulate me, beyond her usual actions to bring out the best in me, or so she claimed, there were a lot of things that didn't make sense.

"Now, we know the grimoire was brought back to Orrin for a reason." Claudia's eyes met mine. "I'm glad Reverend Mother Hózhó isn't taking Reverend Mother Alara's word at face value."

"So what do you need us to do, Anthea?" Ben asked.

"For now, keep your ears open—" I was interrupted by the colorful blanket over the doorway being drawn back.

The Diné Balance chief warden said something, but my wards muffled her voice to the point of incomprehensibility. I gestured for her to wait a moment and mumbled the spell to drop my wards.

"Forgive me, Chief Warden," I said. "What do you need?"

She grimaced. "Your presence is requested by the full Nation Council, Chief Justice," she said in stilted Issuran.

Migina leapt to her feet. "She's not anywhere without an escort."

Gina peered over the chief warden's arm and grinned. "That's what I told her."

"All eight of your guards are here to protect you, Lady Justice," the chief warden said.

I stood. "Then let's not keep your council waiting."

Chapter 21

I can't say I was worried as I and my guard strode toward the Matriarch's Residence. The chief warden hadn't asked me or any of the wardens or peacekeepers to disarm themselves prior to talking to the council. If Reverend Mother Hózhó decided to truthspell me, I would object. There simply wasn't enough probable cause to charge me with murder.

We entered the Matriarch's Residence, and the low rumble of voices from the gathered Diné leaders immediately ceased. In Issura, such a silence didn't bode well. I hoped Gina was right, and it was merely the attention one granted a guest in Heart.

I glanced at her on my right, and she gave me the minutest shrug of her left shoulder. So she wasn't sure what was going on either.

"We are here to serve." I bowed to the Matriarch, and my entourage followed suit.

"For that, we are blessed by the Twelve," she replied. "Is your offer to assist the Reverend Mother of Balance in her investigation still valid?"

"Of course, Matriarch." I glanced in the direction of their Reverend Mother of Death. "However, your people may find some of my methods and questions unorthodox. I mean no disrespect, Matriarch, but is the purpose in my assistance to find the truth or to assuage someone's ego?"

The amount of gasps and titters at my audacity seemed equal among the Diné leadership. However, the Matriarch pursed her lips. I definitely hadn't made any friends there.

But on the other hand, I was very tired of being used by nearly everyone around me. Given her attitude during this morning's meeting, I had to wonder if she was setting me up for something.

"Very well," she said brusquely. "The Reverend Mother of Death will show you the body."

"May I ask for additional assistance?" I forced myself to breath evenly and calmly.

A perturbed expression filled the Matriarch's visage. "Who will you need?"

"High Brother Luc, Sister Claudia, and Sister Migina from my party," I rattled off. "Plus, volunteers from your Light and Death Temples as well as a volunteer from your Healers Guild."

"You don't ask for much, do you, Chief Justice?" Reverend Mother Hózhó commented dryly. "Don't you wish assistance from Balance?"

"I beg your pardon, Reverend Mother." I inclined my head. "I assumed you and your justices would be taking the lead in this investigation."

She snorted. "That's the first non-insulting thing you've said since you've come in here, Chief Justice."

"My apologies, Reverend Mother, but as my own Reverend Mother pointed out to you, discretion is a talent I sorely lack," I replied.

"Reverend Mother, may we have members of other Temples observe as well," Reverend Father Kilchii said.

Reverend Mother Hózhó turned toward his relative direction. "Making this a family affair, Kilchii?"

"Considering three of my offspring worked very well together in Tandor to root out demon spies, I would think you would want the best working on your investigation," he replied.

"If we're going to have a large number of people observing, is there someplace besides Death's morgue we may use?" I asked.

The Reverend Mother of Death scowled at me. "You will not disrespect the dead, Chief Justice."

"I have no intention of disrespecting anyone, Reverend Mother." I looked up at the logs supporting the entryway before I turned back to her. "Do you have a suggestion on how the deceased managed to access the ceiling of the entryway? I didn't see any ladders when Warden Dezba and I arrived after the discovery was made."

Despite my respectful tone, the Reverend Mother of Death continued to scowl at me. "Discovering that is your task. However, the body will not leave Death. Since you seem quite adamant in bringing up demons using human skins to disguise themselves, and your extensive experience with said demons, you have until sundown tomorrow to complete your investigation. Hózhó, don't make me lodge a formal complaint that your order deliberately delayed the burning of a corpse."

"I trust Chief Justice Anthea and I will be finished by then." Reverend Mother Hózhó smiled in the general direction of the disgruntled head of the Temple of Death.

I prayed to Balance I could live up to Reverend Mother Hózhó's expectations.

First thing I did was to request everyone clear the council room and the entryway of the Matriarch's Residence. No one really argued since it was well past everyone's normal bedtime. The second was to send Mylon and one of the peacekeepers back to Balance to gather the requested clergy. My other three wardens and Peacekeeper Leyti spread out and examined every nook and cranny of the two areas.

"Who was the decedent?" I asked Reverend Mother Hózhó. One of her junior Justices, a woman close to my age named Mosi, had eagerly volunteered to assist in the investigation.

"He was Sike, the eldest brother of Johona, leader of the Burning Arrow Clan." The Reverend Mother's voice was grim. "She was Nascha's rival for Matriarch."

"Is that rivalry going to cause problems if we're leading the investigation?" I asked.

The Reverend Mother chuckled. "That's why you were put in charge. You may be one of us through your parents, but since you were raised in Issura, the clan elders agreed you don't have a vested interest in the outcome."

"Well, isn't that . . . wonderful." I crossed my arms. I should have known there was a catch in the Diné Council's request.

Gina stalked over to us, irritation spiking from her. "This isn't good, Chief Justice," she murmured. "There was too much time between the discovery of the body and now, and the scene wasn't adequately secured. Key evidence could have been removed or destroyed."

"I know, Warden." I sighed. "We'll simply do what we can with what evidence we find."

Gina snorted. "The rope our victim was swinging from is the only thing in the entryway we haven't checked." She waved at the hemp knotted to the support timber overhead. "I'll see if I can find a ladder."

"What evidence are you looking for?" Reverend Mother Hózhó asked after Gina trudged further into the Residence. Both the Reverend Mother and Justice Mosi seemed genuinely interested in what we was doing.

"Anything odd or doesn't match," I replied. "Sometimes, we don't know until we find it."

"What does your warden mean by securing a scene?" Mosi asked.

"To keep anyone, including our own people, from destroying

evidence where a crime has occurred, the wardens or peacekeepers keep people back until the magistrate and I can investigate."

"Your wardens and peacekeepers would destroy evidence?" Mosi's surprise tickled my mental shields.

I smiled even though the other justices couldn't see my expression. "Not intentionally. It's more of a matter of keeping well-meaning civilians from accidentally contaminating or destroying any evidence."

Gina and a member of the Matriarch household staff returned with a ladder long enough to reach the ceiling.

"Don't you rewind time to discover the culprit?" Mosi asked.

"I do, but the demons and—" I managed to stop myself from saying "skinwalkers". "—our, um, other opponents have discovered how to set trap spells in the past. We've learned to thoroughly check a corpse and the surrounding area before casting the rewind spell."

"Not to argue semantics, Chief Justice, but all spells are cast in the past unless you are casting in the present moment." Reverend Mother Hózhó sounded more confused than argumentative.

"I do not dispute your logic, Reverend Mother." I watched as Long Feather and Leyti helped Gina and the staff member place the ladder against the rafters in order to examine the end of the rope still tied to the ceiling support log. "However, in doing a rewind, you can place physical objects or spells in the past. Or those same things can be yanked forward in time."

"So, technically, the spell is not here at this moment because you will yank it forward further down the timeline." Mosi waved her fingers as if working out the spell in her mind.

The four people anchored the bottom of the ladder while Dezba scrambled up the rungs.

"That's our understanding in Orrin," I said. "Chief Justice Elizabeth and Justice Yanaba were experimenting with the concept, but the depletion of bodily resources has been too much for Justice Yanaba in the second half of her pregnancy, so they halted their experiments for now."

"Don't even think about it until after you deliver your child, Mosi," the Reverend Mother chided gently.

"But this confirms Chief Justice Haben of D'mt's theory that time isn't like a river, flowing in the same direction. Time, and therefore, *we* can move in different directions, not just forward!" Mosi's excitement was contagious even though we were in the middle of a potential murder investigation.

"Chief Justice Haben's theory?" I said.

"Surely, you've read her treatise?" Mosi cocked her head. "Isn't that where you got the idea to place the flashbang in Tandor's tunnel system in the past?"

"Frankly, I pulled that idea out of my arse in desperation." I chuckled. "How in Balance did you hear about that?"

"Brother Bumblebee told me about it." Her hands brightened to a brilliant red, and she tucked them in the sleeves of her robes.

I couldn't resist teasing her a little. "Actually, Justice, I'm pleased to hear my younger brother can share pillow talk." I lowered my voice and leaned closer to her hood. "Too many of the Light priests have no clue of what they are doing in bed."

Mosi snorted and slapped her hands over her mouth to contain a full-on guffaw.

"High Brother Luc was right. Your sense of humor can be quite annoying," Reverend Mother Hózhó commented.

"Could I get that in writing, Reverend Mother?" Luc swung to a halt beside me on his crutches. "So rarely does any justice admit I'm right about something."

"What can we do to help?" Claudia said. I hadn't heard her bells because she wasn't wearing her formal robes. Instead she wore the warrior's gear she had on the journey to Diné. A scarf tied around her head kept her short curls out of her face.

"You and Sister Migina have been involved in investigations in Orrin before." I smiled at her. "Between your sharp mind and her sharp eyes, I'm hoping we can conclude this case quickly."

"Warden Mylon said the Reverend Mother of Death gave you until sundown," Luc said softly.

"Only as far as examining the body," I replied. "She's adamant that it be burned properly."

"Chief Justice," Dezba called down. "The rope has been tied in a water bowline knot."

I looked at the Reverend Mother and Mosi. "Do your people use that knot often?"

"I've never heard of it," Reverend Mother Hózhó said.

"Neither have I," Mosi added.

I looked back up at my warden, who reached for the rope. Dread and suspicion struck, or maybe it was simply too much experience. I screamed, "Don't touch it, Dezba!"

My warning was too late. The force of the spell struck her. She teetered on the rung for a heartbeat before she plummeted toward the hard packed earthen floor.

Chapter 22

My heart lodged in my throat. Out of instinct, I threw out my hands and froze the time around Dezba. She hung in midair, a look of resignation on her face.

"What in Light?!" It wasn't Luc's voice.

"Someone grab her and lay her on the floor," I yelled. "I can't hold her forever!" Sweat already beaded all over my body at the strain and lack of preparation.

Gina and Leyti shook themselves out of their shock. She scrambled up a couple of rungs and pushed Dezba's frozen form toward Leyti's outstretch hands. Together, they carefully placed her on her back on the earthen floor.

I released the spell and bent over double. Nausea mixed with great gasping lungfuls of air as I tried not to pass out.

Dezba rolled over and began vomiting. Luc and Claudia hurried across the room to check on her. The odd thing was the lack of a response inside me at seeing them work together. Maybe my time with Mya at Child had been a good thing after all.

"Are you all right, Anthea?" Reverend Father Kilchii said behind me.

"I will be." I gasped and straightened as my blood slowed its pounding in my head. Someone rubbed my back. I look over my shoulder to

126

see the female Thief priestess who had accompanied us the last day of our journey.

"Greetings," she said in Issuran. She smiled as she continued her ministrations. "I am Shideezhi."

I glanced at Reverend Father Kilchii. "It is a pleasure to meet you, Younger Sister," I replied in Diné before I switched to Issuran. "You must take after our father in playing word games."

She laughed, a bell-like feminine sound and dropped her hand from my back. "So what does Anthea mean in Issuran?"

My mouth twisted. "My name is actually from the Greek city-states. It means 'blossom.'"

"Would you prefer I call you Shadi?" She seemed to have a sense of humor even more perverse than mine.

"You might want to stick to Anthea." I grinned. "There may be more older sisters of yours running around."

Shideezhi laughed hard. "I like you, sister. A pity we didn't meet until now."

I shook my head. "We should never have known of each other at all. But I find myself regretting not growing up with you." And I meant it. I envied Luc that his little sister still wrote to him from Cant.

Having caught my breath, I strode over to my fallen warden. A master healer tended to Dezba, but her skin still had a sickly greenish-yellow color. "Warden, how many times do I have to tell you to watch where you put your hands?"

"I was looking at where I was placing my hands." Her grin was interrupted by a wave of nausea that nearly made me lose the sweet corn cakes I'd eaten earlier.

Luc looked at me and rolled his eyes. "She's suffering from magic backlash, but otherwise, she'll recover."

"Thank you for keeping me from landing on my head, Chief Justice," Dezba whispered.

"What did the spell do to you?" I asked.

"It felt like static, but far more powerful." Dezba closed her eyes, trying to get her stomach back under control. "It surprised me more than injured me."

The healer said something in Diné to us. Her statement was far beyond my meager language skills. I only caught a handful of words.

"She said Dezba's heart rate is erratic," Gina translated for us. "She wants to take her back to the Healers Guild to have her watched overnight. The healer will return to the Residence once her journeywoman has been briefed."

I nodded before I said, "Thank you," in Diné.

The healer smiled and nodded in return. Apparently, I scored some good will with the master healer.

Dezba waved her hands. "Before I get dragged to the Healers Guild, Chief Justice, you need to know the knot tied was a water bowline."

I narrowed my eyes as I looked up. I couldn't make out the exact knot from here, but I trusted her observation.

"I don't understand the significance," Reverend Father Kilchii murmured.

"It's a common sailors' knot along the Peaceful Sea," I replied. "You don't live in the second largest port of Issura without picking up certain things."

"And it's not used here in Diné," Dezba added.

"Why would you mention it?" Justice Mosi along with Reverend Mother Hózhó, Brother Bumblebee, Sister Shideezhi, and High Brother Pecos had joined us. "It points the blame at you Issurans."

"Exactly," I said. "Who would benefit from causing trouble between the Matriarch and Elder Johona by killing her brother? And who would benefit by causing trouble between Issura and Diné?"

"Are you that sure of your people?" Reverend Mother Hózhó aimed her sightless eyes in my general direction.

"The chief justice and I hand-picked most of them." Luc used his crutches to lurch to his foot. "The ones we didn't were recommended by their seats or the magistrate, all of whom we trust. In the case of Lady Alessa, her brother, the Duke of Orrin, put his life on the line by swearing responsibility for Chief Justice Anthea's behavior when she was found guilty of an action she should have been praised for. Plus, the chief justice and I are godparents to the duke's heir."

"So you brought family with you?" the Reverend Mother asked.

"Yes," Luc and I said at the same time.

"Very well, then. What do you propose next?"

I looked up at the ceiling. "First we retrieve the rope. I want to know what kind of spell was laid on it that didn't affect the people who cut down Sike's body. Then we'll do the rewind."

After four wardens carried Dezba to the Healers Guild building and the remaining assistant investigators argued their cases furiously, High Brother Pecos climbed the ladder to retrieve the rope knotted around the support timber. Somehow, he was able to balance on the ladder and pry the knot open with the tips of two knives. Maybe his balancing skill came from fighting on horseback.

Once the rope was secured in a clean silk bag Justice Mosi brought with her, Reverend Mother Hózhó cleared the area of everyone who was not a justice or an experienced rewind witness.

I sat with the other two justices in a circle on the floor between the entry and the council room. Apparently, the Reverend Mother had done a threshold rewind spell before in order for her witnesses to see what happened in two rooms at the same time. When I mentioned my disappointment I hadn't discovered a new technique, she made a disgusted sound low in her throat and said, "It sounds like Reverend Mother Alara has been remiss in the training of her novices."

I couldn't dispute her assessment. Maybe once this investigation into Sike's death was over, we'd have a chance to learn more from each other.

Together, the three of us said the words of the spell, grasped the threads of time and yanked them back to First Evening when the feast started. As I'd noted before, a rewind was easier when I did it with another justice. It was a pity there were so few of us.

Not that I'd wish blindness on anyone. I never understood why Balance used our loss of sight as an indicator of Her favor. Not that She would ever deign to explain such things to me.

We let the timelines slide forward slightly faster than how we experienced it.

"Staff are carrying food from the Residence's kitchen to the gathering," Luc reported. "Slower. I've spotted Sike. He's speaking with the Matriarch."

These are the times when I wished we had sound to go with the observations in a rewind. Though if the visual aspect was translucent to those with normal sight, the sound would probably be distorted as well.

"She looks embarrassed and pleased by whatever he is saying." Luc's voice had a baffled quality. "The Matriarch leaves the building, but Sike turns and goes into the residential section."

I could feel Reverend Mother Hózhó and Mosi's bewilderment in our link. Was Sike courting his sister's political rival?

"Continue," Luc called out.

We let the slippage of time speed up. Even working with two other justices, my small clothes grew damp with perspiration. The armpits of my silk shirt was already soaked from my earlier efforts. I forced myself to concentrate on the spell instead of a need for a bath.

"Fewer people are leaving the Residence," Bumblebee added. "Now there's no one in the council hall."

"Slow!" Luc shouted. "Can anyone identify this woman?" Gina repeated his question in Diné. There was a series of negative responses in both languages.

"She's carrying Sike over her shoulder through the council hall," Luc continued. "He's either unconscious or dead. What the demon?!"

"Witness!" Reverend Mother Hózhó demanded.

"She has dropped Sike on the floor in the entryway," Bumblebee choked out. "Now she's crawling up the wall like an insect."

"Or a demon," Pecos added.

"She's tying the rope to the support beam," Luc said. "She's laying the spell on it."

Gasps and other sounds of shock came from the people around us.

"She has extruded two tentacles from her mouth," Luc reported in a shaky voice. "The tentacles lift Sike to the entity's main body. It ties the noose around his neck and lets him drop. His body sways at the end of the rope. The entity climbs down the wall again and dashes from the room."

Gina muttered a Cantan curse. "She's fast. Demon fast."

"Three staff members enter the building with empty serving dishes," Bumblebee continued. "One of them activates the Light globes. Her middle companion screams at the sight of Sike. The other two look up and scream as well."

"People are running in from the dance," Leyti added. "They stop and stare. The chief justice and Warden Dezba push their way to the front of the crowd."

"The entity who hung Sike enters from the east doorway." Luc shuffled across the room as he followed the ghostly past image of our assailant. "She is talking to the other spectators and pretending to be shocked."

"The Matriarch enters," Bumblebee continued. "She gives the order for the foreign visitors to be taken to the Temples. Wardens clear the civilians from the room."

"Our assailant is escorted along with the rest of the staff out the eastern doorway," Luc added. "I wish Lailani was here so we could try to find out who she is."

"A ladder is brought in. Niyol climbs it and cuts down Sike's body." Bumblebee sounded more shaken now than when we were fighting demons hand-to-hand in the streets of Tandor. "Niyol has no reaction to touching the rope. The Death clergy wrap the body and carry it out of the Residence."

"A few groups including the Matriarch are having discussions," Gina said. She cleared her throat. "Only she and Reverend Father Kilchii remain. She's having difficulty maintaining her composure. He hugs her. They part abruptly when Johona enters the Residence. The two women hug."

"More elders and Temple seats enter the Residence," Leyti said. "They start their council."

"Lady Justices, you can go faster now," Luc said.

We sped the flow of time until the past slid into the now. My eyes burned, and I blinked the sweat out of them. Mosi shook the feeling back in her hands. The Reverend Mother simply looked angry.

"We need a picture of this person to circulate among the civilians and Temples," I murmured. "Does anyone in our party draw?"

"Mylon does," Long Feather volunteered as he helped me to my feet. Two of the Diné Balance wardens assisted their justices.

"Mylon?" I stared at Long Feather.

"Yes, m'lady." He grinned. "Who do you think taught Lailani?"

I was glad Long Feather had a firm grip on my elbow. Otherwise, I would have surely fallen at his revelation.

Chapter 23

While Long Feather and my younger siblings worked with Mylon to create an accurate description of the entity who hung Sike in the Matriarch's residence, Luc and our entourage accompanied us to the Temple of Death. The Diné healer joined us on the way, and she brought her apprentice with her.

My younger siblings. Bumblebee. Shideezhi. Pecos.

Eighteen months ago, my only known family was my birth mother Gerd. Now . . .

Now, I had far more relatives than I knew what to do with, and that wasn't counting my great-grandmother's clan. And surprisingly, none of them were trying to kill me.

Are you really all right? Luc asked silently as we walked. *I don't wish to insult you, but you look like you might still get sick to your stomach.*

I picked up the symptoms of Dezba's magic backlash. I smiled wryly at Luc. *It serves me right for not instructing her about the rope before she climbed up there.*

He frowned. *You think you were the target of the spell, don't you?*

I know this sounds conceited, but yes. I shrugged. *It would explain why Niyol and Pecos weren't affected, and why Dezba received only a mild shock. She's not a passive, but she's been around Balance magic most of her life. It's reasonable to assume exposure to magic would leave some kind of mark on a person, like how the sun can affect human skin.*

You think it would have affected your lightning abilities?

Yes, but what's worse is I can't control them. I sighed. *Novices of Mother and Father have been known to accidentally set themselves on fire while trying to master their abilities. I'm frightened enough of killing someone trying to master lightning. That spell might have triggered my talent and killed everyone present.*

Why don't you consult with Sister Lizard? he suggested. *She might know where to find any record of someone having that talent.*

I grinned at him. *When we get a candlemark without chaos, I plan to ask her.*

Why kill you now if the renegades think they've converted you? Luc asked.

It may be a test to see if they succeeded, just like the alleged letter from Reverend Mother Alara, I grumbled.

Luc paused for less than a heartbeat and stared at me before he resumed his pace. His worry rubbed roughly against my psyche. *You can't seriously be thinking of using these tests to find a way to infiltrate the renegades.*

Why not? I snapped. *They went to great lengths to get that blasted grimoire back into my hands to corrupt me.*

Because you're not that good of an actor. His dry humor tickled my mind. I wasn't sure whether to laugh along with him or be irritated at his estimation of my abilities.

However, I made the effort to show a serious and contrite mein as an ambassador should when we entered the Temple of Death. Their sanctuary felt warmer with the green sandstones, but the basalt statue of Death with her arms held out in welcome looked very similar to the one back in Orrin. My proper attitude didn't erase the scowls from the Reverend Mother or any of her clergy.

"The body should have been bathed by now," she snapped.

"If Sike had died of natural causes or accidental injury, I would not have asked you to delay your duties, Reverend Mother," I murmured. "Frankly, I dislike this aspect of my Temple's responsibilities, but I want Sike's murderer brought to justice. Don't you?"

"You're assuming he was murdered." The sneer in her voice matched the one on her face.

I pushed back my hood and raised my right eyebrow at her statement. "Are the Diné prone to taking their own lives in such a public manner?"

My inquiry caught her off guard. "Of course not."

"Are you saying Reverend Mother Hózhó and her staff cannot properly conduct a rewind spell?"

The Reverend Mother of Death shuffled her feet. Her clergy coughed and muttered among themselves. They may not have understood our words, but they could understand the tone. The Reverend Mother barked something at them. Something that was obviously an insult aimed at me.

"Warden Gina, would you translate my words to everyone present?" I inclined my head to the Reverend Mother of Death. "I do not wish there to be any misunderstandings while I'm here in Heart as a representative of Queen Teodora as well as the Temple of Balance."

Thankfully, Gina kept a straight face and repeated my words in Diné. Reverend Mother Hózhó bowed her head, her hood covering her face. There were no emotions coming from her, but I had the distinct impression she struggled to hold in her laughter.

The master healer stepped forward and spoke. Gina translated her words. "What do you need from me, Chief Justice?"

"Is Sike's neck broken?" I asked.

The healer moved to the head of the corpse and manually examined it. She shook her head. "If one of the first five vertebrae is broken, it is merely cracked, and it hasn't injured the spinal nerve cord." The healer glanced at the Reverend Mother of Death before she looked at me. "Of course, the only way to confirm my hypothesis is to examine the bones directly."

At the healer's last statement, the Death clergy made the same hissing sound the Matriarch made when I brought up the subject of skinwalkers. This was going to be a lot harder than dealing with High Brother Xander, and High Sister Bertrice before him.

"Please do not attack your own healer," I said. "I have not asked for an internal examination of Sike's body, nor did she volunteer to do so."

"She said the only way to confirm her hypothesis was to cut open the body," the Reverend Mother of Death spat.

"That is not what she said," Reverend Mother Hózhó said quietly. "Or would you like me to truthspell you here and now?"

"You have no cause!" The skin of the Reverend Mother of Death practically glowed red. I didn't need the sharp jabs at my psyche to confirm her mood.

"You just insulted both a visiting justice and one of our own healers by stating they were less than professional." Reverend Mother Hózhó pushed back her hood. Her blank yellow eyes seemed to bore into her counterpart of Death. "That is not just an insult, but slander, a legally actionable offense, and quite frankly, you shame me and our entire nation with your behavior."

The last statement took the air out of the Reverend Mother of Death's sails. Her jaw clenched and released as if the words she were about to say made her physically ill.

"I apologize to you both, Chief Justice and Master Healer." The Reverend Mother of Death inclined her head. "Please continue."

"Master Healer, are there any bruises about Sike's neck?" I asked.

"I need more light," she said.

"Bother Bumblebee, if you would." I gestured at a spot above the table. He manifested a light ball that made a good number of the people present squint.

The healer turned the corpse's head left and right and checked the back of the neck. She straightened and shook her head.

"One last question, Master Healer." I flipped up the part of the sheet covering Sike's toes. "Do the fingertips and toes show any unusual coloring?"

She moved around the table checking the hands and feet of the corpse before she asked a question of her apprentice. He repeated her examination of the corpse's limbs.

"She is using this as a training opportunity," Gina murmured.

"That's good," I whispered. "The Diné justices need all the help they can get."

When the apprentice finished, he said, "There is the bluish discoloration of blood pooling in the lowest parts the body, but I see nothing unusual." He asked something else, but the master healer indicated he should ask me.

"You spoke of unusual coloring, Chief Justice," Gina translated for him. "May I ask what color you were expecting?"

"Cherry red," I answered.

It took Gina a few moments to translate the color I meant. I wanted to kick myself. The Diné didn't have tree fruits like fresh apples, plums or cherries. If they acquired any fruits outside of their domain, they would be dried and a darker shade of their original color.

Finally, my warden got my point across, and the master healer nodded.

"You suspect prussic acid, also called southern blue. It's a favorite poison of the Assassins Guild because of how fast it acts. However, Sike's skin isn't showing the coloring you expected." She stared at the corpse for a long moment. "His assailant could have injected it."

"He's a good-sized man, and an excellent wrestler," the Reverend Mother of Death said. "He wouldn't meekly submit to being stabbed with a poisoned object."

I resisted the urge to grin. The Reverend Mother was intrigued by our investigation despite her entrenched religious objections to what we were doing.

"Are there any puncture marks or scratches?" Luc asked.

The healer and her apprentice checked all sides of the corpse, and the clergy of Death assisted in turning the body for examinations without any prompting. Maybe there was some hope for them after all.

When they couldn't find anything besides a broken callus on the corpse's big toe, the master healer said, "Maybe he inhaled the poison."

"Please explain," I said.

"Inhaling prussic acid fumes causes the heart to stop and results in almost instantaneous death," Gina choked out the translated words. "There wouldn't be time for the victim to react or summon help. If someone put the poison in a steaming mug or lamp oil near Sike—"

Luc and I exchanged looks of horror.

"Reverend Father, the Matriarch—" Before I could finish, he ordered his wardens in Diné, and they all raced out the door of the Temple of Death.

"Anthea, go with them," Reverend Mother Hózhó snapped. "They'll need someone to freeze the air so the Conflict personnel don't breathe the poison as well."

I turned and raced after my father and his men. Gina and Long Feather's boots pounded a half step behind me. I prayed to Thief we got to the Matriarch's Residence before someone accidentally stumbled across the poison.

Chapter 24

Reverend Father Kilchii stopped at the entrance of the Matriarch's Residence and called out. Warden Mylon appeared in the doorway, his sword drawn. He relaxed a hair when he spotted Gina and me.

"A kitchen staff member was found dead in the Matriarch's quarters," he reported. "Brother Bumblebee and Sister Shideezhi ordered the building evacuated. Everyone who was inside is currently on the overlook."

"Please tell us they didn't start any fires," I said.

Mylon shook his head. "One of the Comanche wardens is a weather wizard of modest power. He said he sensed bad air in the Matriarch's personal quarters." His mouth tilted slightly. "High Brother Pecos had to do some fast talking to keep the Matriarch from entering her personal quarters and to smooth the Matriarch's feathers over his warden violating the lady's privacy. Both the brother and his warden are upstairs clearing out the bad air."

Reverend Father Kilchii exhaled gustily. "Thank Conflict, you all kept your heads."

Mylon nodded and stepped out of the doorway. "Sister Shideezhi is guarding the household with Brother Bumblebee and wishes to speak with you and the chief justice as soon as you have reviewed the Matriarch's personal quarters."

Reverend Father Kilchii turned to me. "All your wardens know you well. I thought Tyra was an exception."

"All of my wardens are exceptional," I replied. "Were you able to sketch our culprit from the clergy's descriptions?"

Mylon's skin brightened to a reddish orange at my compliment. "Yes, m'lady. Unfortunately, I was only halfway through drawing a second copy when the Comanche warden raised the alarm."

"My wardens can take over guarding the entrance," Reverend Father Kilchii said. "It's best if you continue your sketches, Warden Mylon. Someone within Heart has to be able to identify this woman." At Mylon's glance at me, the Reverend Father amended his instructions. "Provided you agree, Chief Justice?"

"I'm sorry for sticking you with clerical duties, Warden," I said. "But we do need those pictures."

"Of course, Lady Justice." Mylon bowed. "May I go to the Healers Guild to check on Warden Dezba first? Then I'll return to Balance and work on them."

"Yes, of course," I replied.

Mylon strode out into the night. Reverend Father Kilchii gave more orders to his squad of wardens. They did not accompany us as he gestured Gina and me to follow him.

"I apologize for superseding your authority, Chief Justice," the Reverend Father murmured as we climbed the stairs to the personal quarters on the third floor.

It was my turn to be amused by his formality. "I seem to recall ceding my authority to you in Tandor late last winter, and that was in my queendom. You have every right to expect your authority to be paramount within your own nation."

"But Tandor was war, daughter," he said. "Heart is not under attack."

"Actually, yes, it is," I said gravely.

My father had no reply to my statement.

High Brother Pecos stood outside of a doorway in the middle of the third floor hallway. His eyes were closed, and his hands rested on the shoulders of a Comanche warden who sat cross-legged on the wood plank floor between Pecos and the doorway. I recognized the waving of the warden's hands. They were the same gestures many of the sailors with wind talent used.

Finally, they both opened their eyes, and their shoulders sagged.

"Did it work?" I asked.

Pecos looked down at his warden and repeated my question in their language. The other man nodded and said in Issuran, "Safe."

The warden moved to leaned against the wall. He pulled a piece of jerky from a pocket on his belt and chewed on it. Part of me wished I could do the same.

Light magic exuded from the alabaster sconces, which meant there was sufficient illumination for those with normal human sight to see. Gina entered first and slowly walked around the Diné equivalent of a sitting room, examining objects without touching them. Finally, she nodded.

Pecos, our father, and I followed her into the room. If feminine style along with Diné symbols of power and protection weren't enough to indicate these were the Matriarch's personal quarters, Reverend Father Kilchii's higher body heat confirmed it.

Or maybe it was the dead girl lying in the middle of the room. A wash bowl lay in a large wet spot next to the body on the central rug.

"I think we found our murder weapon," I muttered.

"What is it you tell us wardens and the junior clergy about not jumping to conclusions?" Gina said behind me.

"Take a careful sniff of the air," I said.

She stepped closer to the body and inhaled. "Bitter almonds. Well, damn."

I crossed to the dry right corner of the finely woven wool. "Pecos, help me lift the rug. Whatever you do, don't touch the wet part. You could absorb the poison."

He gave me a skeptical look, but he did as I requested. "What are we looking for?"

Liquid pooled in the unbaked clay packed between the wooden planks. "It doesn't look like any of the poisoned wash water seeped through the floor."

Reverend Father Kilchii nodded sharply. "I'll check the rooms below us, daughter."

After he left, Pecos eyed me from across the rug. "Now that you know about—" He tilted his head to indicate the departed Reverend Father. "Are you upset with me for not saying anything to you when we were trapped in Tandor?"

I cocked my head and straightened. "Why would I be upset with you? It was the Reverend Father who played word games with me."

"I didn't like the fact he did that." Pecos grimaced as he rose to his full height. "But I didn't want to upset you with matters that were irrelevant to our situation. You didn't need any more stress than what we were already experiencing."

"So you made a strategic decision for the best of the city defenders." I smiled at him. "I can't fault you for that."

From behind Pecos, Gina stuck out her tongue at me. Thankfully, she didn't volunteer how I angry I was at the Reverend Father's games. But my father had plotted with my maternal grandmother and her chief warden to spirit me away to Diné. Though their plan failed thanks to me being blind at birth, it meant they both cared about me.

"I'm merely sorry we didn't get to know each other as children," I said. "It would have been nice to have siblings."

"My Comanche brothers and sisters are yours as well as the Diné ones." He grinned at me.

"I'm still getting used to the fact Reverend Mother Hózhó and the

Matriarch are my maternal cousins." I grinned back. "I've been in Heart less than a day. Don't give me more family than I can handle."

"They are?" Gina and Pecos said at the same time.

"Yes." I waved at the dead girl. "Warden, is there any discoloration of her extremities?"

Gina crouched as close as she dared to the corpse. "No, Chief Justice. But there is a small amount of foam around her mouth." She looked up at me. "Seizures aren't uncommon before death in someone poisoned with southern blue."

She examined the corpse again. "What if the demons aren't affected by southern blue?"

"What do you mean?" I asked.

Gina pushed to her feet. "Demon eggs look like sapphires. What if it's because their shells are made of southern blue? It would explain where the Assassins Guild is getting so much of their poison these days."

My stomach churned in a way that had nothing to do with me overextending my abilities or experiencing Dezba's magic backlash. Gina had put together important pieces of the puzzle, but I had no idea how they fit into the rest of our problems.

Chapter 25

The Temple of Death carefully collected the body of the female household staff member and Pecos sent his warden back to the Temple of Conflict to get some rest. He and I gingerly rolled up the rug soaked in poison to allow the wood to dry. We would need water-proofed canvas or leather to remove the rug and wood so no one touched the southern blue.

Gina ran downstairs to find a piece of charcoal. When she returned, she marked the contaminated boards. Finally, she meticulously wrote on the hallway wall in the Diné language, warning anyone from entering the room without express permission from a justice. It wasn't much, but it would have to do. Neither Pecos nor I had the reserves left to ward the room, much less perform a rewind. I would need to borrow one of the Diné justices.

Since the Reverend Father hadn't returned, we took the stairs down to the second floor. We found him in the room beneath the Matriarch's sitting room, staring at nothing. The quarters appeared to be a man's room. Belongings were scattered as if their owner were in a hurry.

"Whose room is this?" Pecos asked.

"Sike's." Gina picked up the shirt lying on the bed. "This was the shirt he was wearing when he last spoke to the Matriarch in the council room."

"He came up to change for the feast." I stepped closer to Kilchii. "Reverend Father, are you all right?"

"Sike didn't deserve this. He was a good man. When he started courting Nascha, I thought it was such a good thing for both of them." Father's voice was distant, as if he observed something else entirely. "He could give her what she wanted, everything I couldn't."

"You are Temple," I said softly. "She had no right to expect you to leave. And obviously, Bumblebee did not suffer because of it. He grew into a fine young man."

Father shook his head and turned his attention to me. "Did you know I expected your mother to leave Issura and come back to Diné with me?"

"It's probably best that she didn't," I commented.

"But she might not have become a skinwalker if she had left Issura." His anguish flowed from him, and my eyes burned with tears in response.

"You don't know that," I said fiercely. "She could have come to Diné and made your life miserable. Considering how many times she's tried to kill me, I can only imagine what she would do to Pecos, Shideezhi, and Bumblebee."

A sad, wry smile crossed his face. "You're assuming they would have been born."

"The world would have been a sadder place if they hadn't," I replied.

His smile widened despite his sorrow. "Do you realize you've been speaking in Diné this entire time?"

I looked at Gina. "I owe that to my teacher."

The four of us reached the first floor. Reverend Father Kilchii sent two of his wardens to summon another justice and Light priest to do the rewinds in the Matriarch and Sike's rooms.

I wasn't sure of the response we'd receive when we strode out to the overlook. The Matriarch sat on a bench next to Elder Johona. They hugged and wept together, but for the most part, everyone simply looked expectantly at us.

I scanned the crowd for the person I was supposed to speak with. A panther sat next to Sister Shideezhi. For a brief, pleased moment, I thought it was Sisquoc, but the panther's entire form was smaller than the former Tandoran Wildling.

I approached them, Gina following me, while the Reverend Father joined the Matriarch and Elder Johona in their grief. "You wished to speak with me, Sister Shideezhi?"

She nodded and switched to Issuran. "Sister Chenoa smelled demon inside the Residence, but nowhere outside."

"So the egg hatched inside the building," Gina murmured.

"Recently, too, if it still has tentacles." I rubbed my chin as the pieces edged together in my mind. "I wish we knew how long it takes a demon to mature after hatching."

"Short of hatching one ourselves and raising it—" Gina made a sharp, slashing motion with her hand at the Diné clergies. "Not that I'm recommending doing any such thing."

"Unfortunately, it means there were more eggs brought to the Northern Long Continent than we originally believed." Shideezhi's expression became somber.

"We need to worry about the hatched demon here first," I muttered.

What's wrong? Luc and Father said silently at the same time.

It was a freshly hatched demon that hung Sike's body from the support beam. I paced around each of the dark fire pits and examined each person. Sister Chenoa accompanied me, sniffing each person, and Gina followed, keeping a hand on her knife pommel. When we completed the entire circuit of the area, I looked down at Chenoa, and she shook her head.

The demon is definitely not on the outlook, I reported.

Farrah and the other Wildlings confirm it hasn't come out the mesa entrance either, Luc said.

It has to still be inside the building, Father added.

That's what we suspect as well, I said. The three of us joined him and the grieving elders.

"Forgive me for intruding, Matriarch, but has anyone passed into Death's embrace prior to my party's arrival at Heart?" I asked.

She sniffed. "May I ask why?"

"Do you think someone else was murdered by the assassin?" Elder Johona said.

"We have several theories, Elder," I murmured. "We are trying to narrow down the possibilities."

The Matriarch nodded. "Elder Chooli passed a week ago. She stayed in Heart over the summer because she didn't think her age would allow her to make the trek to her clan's grazing land. Unfortunately, her family arrived here the day after she passed. Again, why is this important?"

"The assassin may not have had a direct hand in Elder Chooli's death, but I believe they used her death to fuel something else," I replied. The last thing I wanted was to spur a panic.

The Matriarch's eyes narrowed, and I sensed the buzz of silent speech. "My sister is on the other side of this building. She says you think there's a demon in my home."

So much for me starting the panic.

Except it wasn't fear coming from the surrounding people. It was anger.

"Yes, there is a demon," I answered. "But someone had to have brought it here. Would it be permissible for someone to touch your mind to show you the person who hung Sike?"

"It won't be you," she snapped.

"I couldn't if I wanted to, Matriarch." I smiled. "While I can see in a manner of speaking, it's not the same as you do. I was about to suggest one of your own people who attended the rewind."

"I would like to see, also," Elder Johona said.

I gestured to Reverend Father Kilchii and Sister Shideezhi. "However the four of you wish to do this."

After a moment, the Matriarch looked up at the Reverend Father and nodded. Elder Johona patted the surface of the bench for Shideezhi to join her. Each pair joined hands, and they all closed their eyes. Another few moments passed as the clergy showed the civilians their mental images of the alleged woman who hung Sike. I hoped both my father and sister had enough sense to edit their memories of the rewind.

The Matriarch's eyes snapped open, and fury flitted across her features. "The girls from White Water clan!"

"What girls?" I asked.

"You were correct, Chief Justice," she snapped, but her ire wasn't aimed at me. "Two girls from the White Water clan arrived the day before Elder Chooli passed. They requested permission to search for husbands during the upcoming festival."

"Forgive me, but is this unusual?" I asked.

"No." Though the Matriarch was visibly calmer, anger still snapped and cracked along her psyche. "Women are required to pick a mate from one of the other clans who isn't related by four degrees to keep the bloodlines varied. It's good manners to approach the head of the clan before courting one of her male members."

"They also asked my permission," Elder Johona volunteered. "As they did from any other clan leader who has arrived for the winter."

"Including Elder Chooli?" Shideezhi asked.

The Matriarch and Elder Johona looked at each other with alarmed expressions.

"She was the oldest of all the clan elders," Elder Johona said.

"But her clan didn't get here until after Chooli's death," the Matriarch protested.

Elder Johona shrugged. "Neither did mine, but the girls followed tradition and asked me in what I assumed at the time was anticipation of my clan's arrival."

I hugged myself. It sounds more like they were scouting their victims. If Elder Chooli was unwell as the Matriarch said, she would be the easiest victim the White Water girls could use as a sacrifice to hatch the demon egg.

"But why Sike?" the Matriarch said.

"We don't think he was the target." Reverend Father Kilchii still held her hands. "We think you were."

"Killing me would only prompt another council election," she said.

"Not if what they wanted was your skin," I said.

Anthea? Luc's silent question tickle my mind. I could feel Reverend Mother Hózhó with him.

Yes?

Two of the junior justices have completed their rewinds in the Matriarch's sitting room and Sike's quarters.

Let me guess. Our baby demon poisoned the staff member by dropping southern blue into the hot water she'd brought up for cleaning. When she collapsed, Sike heard the noise and ran upstairs where he died inhaling the fumes, too.

I hate it when you deduce what I'm about to tell you before I can, he mocked.

Be careful, I said. *The demon is still in the building.*

We know, Reverend Mother Hózhó interjected. *We're warding each room as we search.*

There's still an assassin in Heart who brought the demon egg here, I added.

The Reverend Father of Light is here with us, Luc said. *We'll deal with the demon. You find the assassin.*

"Well?" Reverend Father Kilchii said.

"Your clergy are doing a room-to-room search of the Matriarch's Residence." I grinned. "I'm going to hunt for the assassin that brought the demon egg to Heart."

Chapter 26

"Where are we going?" Shideezhi asked. She jogged along beside me with Gina, Pecos, and Chenoa.

"Our assassin targeted someone who wasn't in a position to defend themselves in order to get close to someone higher ranked." The hard earth of the mesa's path jarred my feet and leg muscles after spending two and a half weeks on horseback in the desert. "The Healers Guild would serve the same purpose."

Similar to Orrin, the Heart healers didn't live in the building where they treated their patients. The main guild house was surrounded by a series of hoogans for the healers and their families, journeypeople, and apprentices.

I shoved aside the curtain across the doorway into the guild house and squinted. A journeywoman looked up from the text she had been reading by lamplight.

"How may I serve, Chief Justice?" she asked.

"Who is the illest or hurtest person spent the night hut?" I said.

"I beg your pardon?" She cocked her head.

My Diné had floundered in my worry. Shideezhi repeated my question words with the proper grammar. "She wants to know where the most ill or injured person spending the night here is."

"Probably the Issuran Wildling," the journeywoman answered.

151

"He's still sleeping off his healing from this morning which isn't unusual with broken ribs and bruised lungs."

"Where—" I demanded.

A loud *bang* echoed through the hallway behind the journeywoman. It was followed by a shout of pain from Warden Mylon.

I surged past the startled journeywoman and aimed for the most noise. At a cross corridor, I turned to my right in time to see Mylon stumble backward out of a room and strike the opposing wall.

A jagged slash showed past the ripped left sleeve of his uniform tunic. Dark pink droplets ran to his elbow as he shifted his knife to a defensive posture on that side.

A woman jumped out of the same room, her own knife raised to strike.

"You're under arrest," Gina shouted in Diné.

The other woman looked at us. Mylon used the opportunity to shift between her and the window at the end of the corridor.

Realizing she was trapped, she ripped what looked like a bead from her necklace.

Once again, I raised my hands out of instinct and shouted the spell to freeze time around her.

"Get the object out of her hand," I ordered. "Be careful. It's southern blue poison."

Mylon didn't so much as blink. He'd been close enough to the assassin he was enveloped in my spell.

Gina and Shideezhi rushed to the assassin. They divested her of the poison, a demon egg, and all the weapons they could find while I struggled to keep the assassin frozen in place. Shideezhi locked spell-threaded cuffs on the woman's wrists.

Just in time, too. My freeze spell collapsed, and I landed ungracefully arse-first on the wooden floor.

The ugly taste of demon magic hit the back of my throat. It was quickly followed by the tingly heat of Light magic. From the reaction of the other clergy, they felt it, too. The cleanliness of Light erased the sour taste from my mouth.

The assassin glared down at me and spat something in a language I didn't recognize. However, Pecos laughed.

"What did she say?" I asked.

"She said some day your luck will run out, Red Justice." He reached down. I took his hand, and he helped me to my feet.

Someone shuffled behind me, and I turned to find the journeywoman supporting a very wobbly Dezba.

"What the demon is going on—" my warden started before she shouted, "Mylon!"

Gina ran to the giant man, but she couldn't do more than to ease his fall.

Bells started ringing in the guild house, adding to the pounding of my head. The journeywoman dragged Dezba back, and Pecos did the same with me. Shideezhi and Cheona escorted their prisoner away while healers flooded into the area.

All I could do was watch as they worked on Mylon. But in the end, they could do nothing to save him.

Gina held the giant warden as he left our world for Death's realm.

Chapter 27

It turned out there were two demons running around the Matriarch's Residence, the one wearing the skin of the girl allegedly from the White Water clan and a second, even younger demon that hadn't found a skin to wear yet. The conjecture among the clergy with Luc was the demons planned to kill the Matriarch and use her skin.

But it was Mylon's death who drove me to confront Reverend Mother Hózhó.

"Of course, the assassin's knife was poisoned!" I banged my fist on the top of the Reverend Mother's desk. "She killed one of my wardens. That's why I should be included in her interrogation. It's only the second time we've actually caught one of these imbeciles to question."

"May I remind you this is not your jurisdiction, Chief Justice," the Reverend Mother said coolly. "I tolerate your presence because you also happen to be an Issuran ambassador."

I sucked in a deep breath. "I apologize for my outburst, Reverend Mother. It was not my intention to offer insult."

"I know, child." She folded her fingers together. "I grieve with you over the loss of Warden Mylon. He was a good man. Without his concern for his friends, Balance only knows what other harm the assassin could have done. Would you be willing to compromise?"

"It depends on what you mean by compromise," I said.

"I want you to tell me what happened when you questioned the previous assassin you caught, and to give me a list of questions for my interrogation of the prisoner," she said. "In return, you'll leave here with a complete copy of the interrogation from my clerks."

To say her proposal shocked me would be an understatement. "You would bypass, Reverend Mother Alara?"

"We can no longer trust her, but you came to that conclusion some time ago."

"You are asking me to betray my own Reverend Mother." I had to restate it to make sure.

"Yes, I am, Chief Justice, but I'm also asking you to be loyal to your queen."

I lowered myself to my chair once again. While my private suspicions about Reverend Mother Alara had been growing for some time, the urge to defend her rose at the Diné Reverend Mother's criticism.

"If it's any consolation, Anthea, my distrust has more to do with her inability to admit a failure than any belief she's a renegade," Reverend Mother Hózhó said softly.

I made a disgusted sound low in my throat. "I don't think whether she's short-sighted or truly evil matters when the end result is the same." I made my decision in that instant. "The other thing Reverend Father Gray Shadow said in his letter to me was that the watcher he placed within the Issuran home Temple of Balance has disappeared."

"From your tone, it was someone you knew," Reverend Mother Hózhó said.

"Yes," I answered. "But that is beside the point. I understand Queen Teodora's worries and why she wants a clear channel of communication with our neighbors—"

"Would it be all right if my own distance speaker contacted you on a regular basis?" the Reverend Mother asked.

I blinked. "You have one separate from the Matriarch?"

Reverend Mother Hózhó smiled. "You've met her. It's Justice Mosi."

I chuckled. "No wonder she's eager to take on cases. She's never done a circuit, has she?"

"I can't afford to let her." Reverend Mother Hózhó sighed. "As much as I wish I could. However, distance speakers and Light clergy are being actively targeted here as well as in Issura. I would ask you do not spread this information lightly. Few outside of my immediate circle know about her extra talent. Not even my sister knows."

"I won't, Reverend Mother." I just wondered how many more secrets I'd have to keep before this was all over.

Reverend Mother Hózhó and I spent the next two candlemarks going over my interrogation of the man we knew as Brother Mat of Light and how he chose to die by truthspell rather than spill his secrets. I spent another candlemark stamping out all the questions I could think of concerning renegade movements, Assassins Guild targets, and demon habits.

I hated not being involved, but Reverend Mother Hózhó was right. The Diné Nation, much less Heart, wasn't my jurisdiction.

By the time I finished, and Gina and I returned to our assigned quarters, First Morning bells started ringing as we undressed for bed.

"Are you all right?" Gina murmured once we were settled in our beds.

"Not anymore than you are," I said gravely. "You and the rest of the wardens think I joke about you accompanying me, but—" Tears leaked from my eyes, and I swallowed hard. "Sometimes, I think being my wardens is a death sentence for you all."

"You're not the only one who feels guilty." Gina's voice had the same wavering quality mine did. "Aglaia and Tyra were my friends, and Mylon..."

I rose from my bed and climbed into Gina's. I held her until she cried herself to sleep.

The animosity from the Diné Reverend Mother of Death and her clergy toward me collapsed under the dual weight of an assassin and two demons in Heart as well as the loss of my warden. In fact, the Reverend Mother of Death requested I speak of Mylon's character at his funeral. I asked if Gina could in my place since she was far closer to him.

Surprisingly, the Reverend Mother not only didn't protest, but she went out of her way to counsel Gina over my warden's grief. I had to wonder if Little Bear knew about Gina and Mylon. It was something I needed to ask when we returned. Not because I wanted to snoop into my wardens' private affairs, but so I knew how to handle the situation when another warden died in the line of duty.

Because at the rate I was going, my entire original contingent would be gathered by Death within the next three years.

At First Evening, all of the Diné people gathered for the three funerals. Sike was a well-loved figure by more than just the Matriarch. The poor household staff girl was simply in the wrong place at the wrong time. According to the rewind, she took the demon by surprise when she entered the Matriarch's quarters.

The demon would have been smarter to let her go instead of killing her, and subsequently Sike. However, it probably wasn't old enough to think logically. Thank the Twelve, we were essentially dealing with an idiotic toddler.

Gina spoke lovingly and passionately about Mylon. He was an unusual man, gentle and fierce at the same time. Part of me was glad for the journey to Diné which allowed me to get to know him better, but that didn't ease my guilt a bit and made me miss him even more.

Reverend Mother Hózhó interrogated the assassin after letting her stew in the dark in the Balance gaol for three days. True to her word, the Reverend Mother gave me two copies of her clerk's record of the interrogation.

Most of the information assisted Diné and the Plains Nations in tracking down traitors and demon eggs within their people. Thank Balance, only two dozen of the blasted eggs made it through Kulshra'jek Pass last spring.

Unfortunately, the assassin knew nothing about renegade activities in Issura. She could only give a description of the contact who brought her the eggs. The woman she sacrificed to hatch the first egg and provide a skin for her was her sister whom she hated. When White Water clan arrived at Heart later in the same day of the interrogation, none of them could identify the assassin, and the assassin herself knew nothing of her parents' origins. She claimed she and her sister had grown up in the guild, and they had no other allegiance.

In the end, Reverend Mother Hózhó allowed me to witness both the trial and execution of the assassin. Neither was as satisfying as I'd hoped. In fact, the whole thing made me rather sad.

The following week allowed me to deal with the other reasons I'd come to Diné to discuss with the Matriarch, like a joint defense city within the Valley of the Lost. Lady Alessa was a huge help in hammering out the details, as well as the modifications to the trade agreements with more time for Issura to make payments for Diné assistance during the Battle of Tandor.

What surprised me the most was when Reverend Father Kilchii requested the presence of my siblings and me for a private observance of the Day of Death.

Dezba had taken Gina to Dezba's clan gathering two days prior. Both women made a huge deal over their absence in front of Luc. So he took advantage of their absence to visit me with the excuse of discussing business.

For once, things came no where close to physical intimacy. We drank tea while we talked about the finalization of the trade deals.

When a lull occurred because we didn't have other things to occupy us, he said, "Do you wish me to leave?"

"No." I held out my right hand. To my relief, he clasped it. "I need to ask your advice as a friend."

"Go on."

I told him about Reverend Father Kilchii's invitation. "I'm not sure why I feel so uneasy over this. When I was a child, I had dreams of my biological father coming and rescuing me from Balance."

"I remember you telling me this years ago." He smiled and squeezed my hand. "Have you even considered this is Balance giving you a measure of your heart's desire after everything Gerd put you through?"

"That's what I'm scared of," I whispered. "That it'll all be yanked away like Kam or my wardens."

"You want guarantees, Anthea," Luc murmured. "Life isn't a guarantee of happiness. It only offers you the possibility of it. Spend time with your father and siblings and get to know them while you can. You won't regret it."

"Thank you." I smiled. While the anxiety was still there, my heart felt a little lighter.

Chapter 28

I had packed the formal chiton, shawl, and sandals Sivan had ordered for me after Justice Yanaba had destroyed my wardrobe, along with everything else in Orrin's Temple of Balance, while I was in Tandor.

When the Day of Death arrived, Gina graciously helped me with my hair. While she didn't have all the accoutrements Sivan had used when I called a convocation a few months ago, Gina wove my braids into a Diné warrior's bun. I questioned her choice, but Dezba assured me the style was appropriate for the occasion, especially since my father was the head of the Diné Temple of Conflict.

For the first time in ages, my wardens allowed me to walk somewhere by myself. The mesa was fairly silent other than the whistle of the wind. The ceremony and vigil at Death wouldn't take place until First Night, so most people napped or talked quietly about those they lost in their homes. No business was conducted on the Day of Death. It was considered bad luck by the superstitious, and simply bad taste by the rest.

I entered the Temple of Conflict and was greeted by the head of household.

He bowed. "The Reverend Father is expecting you, Chief Justice."

"After everything that's happened over the last fortnight, he doesn't post wardens at your entrance?" I asked.

The head of household chuckled as he led me down the corridor leading to the clergy's private quarters. "We have patrols on the borders of our territory, there are lookouts along the edges of the Heart, and guards at both the top and bottom of the tunnel. The only people here right now besides myself are the Reverend Father and his children. What is there to protect us from?"

He had a point.

The head of household pulled back the weaving that served as doors here and announced my presence. I entered to find Pecos and Bumblebee already here, perched on finely woven rugs by a low table. Reverend Father Kilchii rose from the rug where he sat.

"Do you need anything else, Reverend Father?" the head of household asked.

"No, thank you," Reverend Father Kilchii said. He hugged me as his assistant left, and I awkwardly returned the gesture. It was the first time we'd really touched since Tandor. Ever then, it wasn't the same because I didn't realize the truth.

He led me to the rug on the right of where he'd been sitting. In Issura, it would have been a place of honor. I carefully lowered myself into a sitting position next to Pecos.

When Father took his seat, he smiled. "Thank you for coming."

I inclined my head. "The honor is mine."

Pecos laughed. "Can't Issurans let go of their oh-so-formal manners just this once?"

My mouth twisted. "I'm usually lectured for not sticking to our oh-so-formal manners."

Shideezhi burst past the cloth covering the door. She wore cotton skirts and a tunic with a shawl about her shoulders as well. Short doeskin boots covered her feet. Then I realized the men weren't wearing Temple uniforms either.

"Sorry, I'm late—" She spotted me, and a gleeful smile spread across her face. "You came!"

She practically danced over to Pecos and slapped his shoulder. "Move over. You and Bumblebee have had your time with Anthea. I want to get to know her, too."

Pecos chuckled and scooted to the next rug. Shideezhi dropped next to me and gave me an enthusiastic hug.

"Finally, a sister!" she squealed. "Between Mother and Father, all I have are brothers."

"Don't let her fool you, Anthea," Bumblebee said. "We have several female cousins we grew up with." He cocked his head. "Then there was the time when I was too little to know better, she tried to convince me I was *berda*."

"You what?" Father paused in placing plates of food on the table and both of his eyebrows rose.

Bumblebee had me laughing until I was crying over the tricks Shideezhi pulled on him when they were children. Then Father said the prayer for our family members who had passed before us.

Like the rest, I filled my plate and placed a bite of each item in the bowl next to me. An offering for the dead. I bit into the sweet corn cakes that had become my favorite here. They were equally good cold as they were hot.

"Reverend Father, may I get your cook's recipe for these before I leave?" I asked.

He eyed me. "It's 'Father', or if you don't feel ready for that yet, then 'Kilchii'," he said gently. "And yes, you may."

"Thank you . . . Father." Saying the word out loud was strange and comforting at the same time. I'd never had anyone to call "father" before.

Shideezhi nudged me with her elbow. "Tell us about your mother."

I froze. It was the Day of Death, but I couldn't mourn Gerd, much less honor her. Not after everything she'd done.

Father made a low growl of warning deep in his throat.

I held up my hand. "It's all right. Shideezhi doesn't know." I turned to my sister. "I'm going to honor Diné and not speak of certain cultural taboos, but if you truly wish to know, come to Balance in three days, and I will tell you about her."

"I-I'm so sorry." She enveloped me in another hug. "Sit with me and my mother tonight at the formal observance. She would be honored to call you daughter."

I hugged Shideezhi back, and I found myself not wanting to leave Diné.

"Who would you like to remember?" Father said gently.

"If you don't mind, tell me about Chief Justice Thalia," I said. "Tell me about my grandmother."

Chapter 29

Four days later, I collapsed next to Luc on his bed in the guest quarters of Light. Despite the chill air of late fall on the mesa, we were both covered in sweat.

"I wish we could stay here," I murmured.

"You do seem happier in Diné." He rolled on his side to look at me. "Are you thinking of asking for a transfer?"

My sharp bark of laughter caught us both by surprise. "Like the Reverend Mother would ever agree to that."

His fingers traced the trickles of sweat across my breasts and abdomen. "Between highly placed family members, you could probably force her hand."

"But do we leave the queen unguarded with Thief as her only weapon to defend herself?" I grabbed his hand and kissed the palm. "Like you said last year on the way to Nasdine, I can't shirk my duties no matter how much I dislike them."

"It's not a question of shirking your duties," he said. "You have a deep-seated need to do what is right and just. It's one of the reasons I love you."

And his kiss repeated everything he had just said.

If you are enjoying the adventures of Anthea and the people of the Justice universe, drop me a line through my website, on Twitter @Suzan_Harden, or SuzanHardenWriter on Facebook. Recommending the Justice series to your friends or writing a review would be even better.

While Anthea and Luc have proven their mettle as diplomats and strengthened the bonds with Issura's immediate neighbor, matters take a horrible turn for their friends from the Jing Empire. Turn the page for a sneak peak at the next Justice novel, *A Measure of Knowledge*!

A Measure of Knowledge

Chill winter rains had settled over the city of Orrin, and everyone who didn't have to be out in the drizzles and downpours stayed close to their fireplaces and braziers. Those same storms had halted ship traffic in and out of our harbor, and the weather made it too dangerous for the fishers to launch their smaller boats. That left repairs and crafts to occupy idle hands.

I found myself with four justices in residence when there had only been me at the Temple of Balance last winter. Justice Erato and Brother Wolf Run, who currently rode circuit in the east side of the Duchy of Orrin, had come to my Temple to resupply in the late fall, but early and deep snows in the foothills forced them to spend the season here rather than Mountain Gate as they'd planned.

However, our visitors were not bored. The bonding of the city's clergy over the difficulties of the last year had led to spending our free time together on the long, dark nights. Each Temple took turns hosting games, story telling, and music except on Rest Day. We'd gather after First Evening, and a competition of a different sort had broken out among our head cooks and chefs over the quality and variety of dishes served.

On this Sixth Day, we were gathered in the sanctuary of the Temple of Thief for a Mill tournament. My head of household Sivan watched

Baby Kosumi so my junior justice Yanaba could attend. I rather suspected it was my assistant's way of suggesting she and my chief warden make their relationship more permanent with a babe of their own.

The pleasant thing about Mill was that everyone from Balance could play. Talbert made a point of creating game pieces of two different types of material so my sister justices could study the board by touch.

I was the odd one, a justice who had vision, though my perception was different from other sighted humans. I perceived differences due to relative heat exuded by the things, people, and animals around me.

"Your move, Anthea." Sister Cedar Grove smirked at me from across our table.

That was the other thing I loved about our gatherings. We agreed to drop all titles for the durations of our entertainment. It was freeing not to have to worry about etiquette and status for a few candlemarks.

"I am aware, thank you," I growled as I stared at the board. Mill was less complicated than chess, but it still required a certain amount of strategy. It didn't help that this was the last game. As the two finalists, Cedar Grove and I were tied at two games apiece. The winner would take the tournament and the prize gold.

No games could be played at Thief without some gambling involved.

The crowd of clergy pressed closer, and secondary betting impinged on my awareness. I saw the trap Cedar Grove was about to spring. The question was finding a way out.

Or maybe I was looking at the problem from the wrong perspective. Maybe I needed to go around. I slid the copper peg into the hole.

Cedar Grove's breath came out in a whoosh.

"Are you all right, my love?" Garbhan's hand was on her shoulder.

She frowned at the board, trying to figure out my plan. Both of her palms rubbed her swollen belly. "I would be if our daughter would stop kicking my lungs."

"Do you concede?" I smirked at her.

She snorted. "To you? Never!" Still, the Thief priestess took her time, which set off another round of wagering among our peers. She took the space I'd expected, and I made my next move.

Her face fell. She had only two moves left. One where she would lose the match and one where she would tie. Cedar Grove had too much pride to deliberately lose.

So did I.

Pandemonium exploded as we inserted our last pegs into their squares. No one was expecting us to tie. The brothers and sisters of Thief were laughing as they took the gambling proceeds to the dais of the statue of Thief in order to count them.

Cedar Grove and I stood and bowed to each other. I stretched my arms over my head, and arched my back to pull out the knots. Garbhan guided her over to the food table. He'd become rather overprotective of the priestess since he'd seeded her womb. I was sure it was difficult not to form an attachment when bringing a new life into the world.

My thoughts dragged my attention to Luc. He stood next to Talbert, and they both grinned like fools. I realized why. After the Temple of Thief took its cut and the prize gold was split between Cedar Grove and me, the remaining coins were being divided between the two high brothers.

I stalked over to them. "What is going on here?"

"Collecting on our bets," Luc said innocently.

"Y-you bet I would lose?" For some reason, his judgement of my skill hurt. I'd never thought of myself as being that competitive.

He leaned on his left crutch and cupped my cheek. "I know you. And I knew you wouldn't lose."

Confusion rippled through me. "B-but—"

"Balance in all things, Anthea," Talbert teased. "You of all people should know that."

I shook my head at them. "You two are—"

"Brilliant?" Luc offered.

"Ingenious?" Talbert said.

"Pains in my backside," I retorted.

But Shi Hua's screams interrupted our byplay. Jeremy cradled the priestess as she collapsed to the marble floor of the sanctuary.

I raced over, knelt next to Shi Hua, and tried to absorb her pain. Fire ripped through my belly as if sharp claws had gutted me. *Breathe with me, Shi Hua. What's wrong?*

It took several moments for the young woman's agony to recede. At first, I feared a complication from childbirth though she'd delivered little Chao nearly four weeks ago. But it wasn't her pain I was feeling. It was someone else's. Someone who had either passed out or died.

"Mei Wen!" Shi Hua gasped between her words and tears. "She tried to—tried to warn me. A demon army has invaded Chengzhou."

GLOSSARY
WORDS AND PHRASES SPECIFIC TO THE JUSTICE SERIES

Anacapa Islands – a series of four islands off the southwestern coast of Issura. Limuw is the largest. Wi'ma is the second largest. Anacapa is the closest to Orrin. Tuqan is the furthest from Orrin.

Apprentice – lowest rank of a trade or craft guild

Berda – gender fluid; someone who does not stick to traditional gender roles

Britannia – Toscan name for a series of islands off the western coast of the Old Continent. The two largest are Eire and Albion. Four hundred years before Anthea's time, the queens of Eire and Albion were losing their battle against the demons. They ordered the islands evacuated and the Temples of Death to launch their last resort spells. The islands are now barren, and no one who steps on them lives for long.

Briton Diaspora – refers to the survivors and their descendants of the evacuation of Britannia who are now scattered around the world

Brother – title for any fully ordained priest of any Temple that accepts men, except for the Temple of Father

Cant – Issura's neighboring nation-state to the south

Chengzhou – the capital of Jing, a nation-state in the western shore of the Old Continent

Chief Justice – title of the highest ranked priestess at a Temple of Balance

Chief [name of trade] – the highest ranking master guild member of a trade in a city or region

The Cradle – according to legend, the continent where Child created the first members of the human race

Duke/Duchess – highest ranking noble of a region

Distance-view glasses – a telescope

Father – title for any fully ordained priest of the Temple of Father

Gilwas – a city in northern Issura

Gray Mountains – a mountain range that runs the entire length of the western side of the Long Continents

The Grand Canal – a human-built canal that passes through the isthmus connecting the Long Continents

The Green Lady Inn – an inn near the Embassy District of Orrin, it has the only entrance/exit to the tunnel system with the city wall that is not a Temple

Guild – a civil organization for a trade or craft

Guild Master – an expert tradesman's rank based on analysis of his/her peers

Healer – a person with the magical ability to heal illness and repair wounds

High Brother – title of the chief priest of a city Temple, except the Temple of Father

High Father – title of the chief priest of a city's Temple of Father

170

High Mother – title of the chief priestess of a city's Temple of Mother

High Sister – title of the chief priestess of a city Temple, except the Temples of Balance or Mother

Iberia – nation-state on the southwestern corner of the Old Continent

Issura – queendom on the western coast of Northern Long Continent; the Peaceful Sea forms its western border with the nation of Pagonia to the north, the nation of Cant to the south, the nations of the Cliffdwellers and Diné to the southeast and the Gray Mountains to the east

Jing – nation-state on the eastern side of the Old Continent

Journeyman/Journeywoman – middle rank of a trade or craft guild

Justice – title for any fully ordained priestess of the Temple of Balance; alternate term of address is Lady Justice

Kemet – nation-state on the northeast corner of the Cradle

Kulshra'jek Pass – a pass through the Gray Mountains adjacent to Pana Valley, mainly used by Comanche traders in the summer on their way west

The Levant – a loose alliance of Phoenician city-states between the Hittite Empire and Kemet on the eastern side of the Middle Sea

The Long Continents – the two continents separating the Peaceful Sea from the Panthalassa Sea, they are connected by a narrow isthmus

The Lost Continent – southern continent between the Peaceful Sea and the Storm Sea. By Anthea's time, the original inhabitants were believed to be slaughtered by demons 500 years before. Sailors from the Sea Peoples and Maurya who landed there after the inhabitants' disappearance reported screams but found no one. Those with magic talents went mad. Not even the priests and priestesses from Child could save them. Those who tried went mad themselves.

Magistrate – elected official of a city or town in Issura who is responsible for civil and criminal law enforcement and the city or town's defense/care in an emergency

Master – senior member of a trade or craft guild; the clergyperson who is primarily responsible for the training of a novice class

Maurya – the southern-most nation of the Old Continent

Middle Sea – shallow sea that separate The Cradle from the Old Continent

Mother – title for any fully ordained priestess of the Temple of Father

National Road – main, paved road through the nation of Issura. It roughly parallels the western coastline.

New Thenos – an island city/state on the eastern coast of the Northern Long Continent

Novice – a person in training to become a priest/priestess of the Twelve

Orrin – third largest city in the queendom of Issura with the second largest port

Pagonia – Issura's neighboring nation to the north

Panthalassa Sea – ocean that separates the Long Continents from the western part of the Old Continent and the Cradle

Peaceful Sea – ocean that separates the Long Continents from the eastern part of the Old Continent, the islands and archipelagos of the Sea Peoples, and the Lost Continent

Peacekeepers – men and women who act as a city's police force. They report to the city's magistrate. They also act as an auxiliary defense force if their city or nation is attacked.

Pimu – one of a series of four islands off the northern coast of Cant

Rambla – a city in northern Cant, its people were used to hatch demon eggs off-screen during the events of *A Modicum of Truth*

Redwood Grove – a fair-sized town in the northeastern section of the Duchy of Orrin. It nestles on a plateau in the foothills of the Grey Mountains near the border with the Duchy of Pana.

Reverend Father – senior-most priest of a Temple order, the leader of that sect in the nation in which he resides

Reverend Mother – senior-most priestess of a Temple order, the leader of that sect in the nation in which she resides

Seat – person holding the highest ranking position of a Temple

Shakya – nation-state in the western portion of the Old Continent, southwest of Jing and northeast of Maurya

Sister – title for any fully ordained priestess of any Temple that accepts women, except for the Temples of Mother and Balance

Standora – capital and largest city of Issura

Storm Sea – ocean bordered by the eastern part of the Cradle, the southern part of the Old Continent, and the western part of the Lost Continent

Tandor – Issuran city that guards the border with Cant and Diné

Temple – a collection of people dedicated to the service of one of the twelve gods; a building that houses such people; the primary place of worship for one of the twelve gods

Tiwan – the capital of Cant

Toscana – nation-state on the southwest section of the Old Continent; location of the first battle against the demons

The Twelve – the collective name for the twelve deities of the Justice universe

Valencia – duchy in the nation-state of Iberia; know for their innovative shipbuilding designs

Valley of the Lost – the desert between Issura, Diné, and the Cliffdweller Territory

Warden – security guard of a Temple, they act as supplementary military personnel in the event of a demon invasion

Mother

Cloak Color – Light blue

Motto – "To give without thought; to forgive with love."

The Temple of Mother is responsible for the teaching of household arts, such as spinning, weaving, food storage and preparation. The order is also responsible for caring for those who have lost their families.

Father

Cloak Color – Dark blue

Motto – "All tools are weapons, and weapons tools."

The Temple of Father is responsible for the constructive arts, such as carpentry and smithing.

Balance

Cloak Color – Black

Motto – "Balance in all things."

The Temple of Balance runs the judicial system. A justice is the judge in criminal and civil cases.

Light

Cloak Color – Medium brown

Motto – "Light brings truth, for without truth, there can be no justice."

The Temple of Light is responsible for codifying contracts and mediating contract disputes. A Light priest also acts as the bailiff for a justice, and is often the one to truthspell a witness or the accused. The Temple of Light also provides military support to a nation's civilian army.

Knowledge

Cloak Color – Gold

Motto – "With patience, knowledge comes."

The Temple of Knowledge is responsible for education and for recording historical events. They essentially act as the library system for the Justice universe.

Thief

Cloak Color – Grey

Motto – "Hiding in plain sight."

The Temple of Thief acts as the intelligence-gathering arm of both the Temples and the civilian leaders. They finance their efforts through gambling dens.

Conflict

Cloak Color – Dark Red

Motto – "Destruction is the necessary evil, for it clears the way for new growth."

The Temple of Conflict focuses on strategy and all martial arts. They are the primary support and teachers of a nation's army.

Love

Cloak Color – Medium Red

Motto – "Pleasure is life."

The Temple of Love are the holy prostitutes. They also deal with sex education and lead the Spring Rituals, the annual fertility rites which were first used to breed as many humans with magical talent as possible. Don't underestimate them. They fight just as hard and as nasty as their fellow clergy in Conflict.

Child

Cloak Color – Light green

Motto – "All things are new once."

The Temple of Child is responsible for the emotional health of citizens. They also develop and teach agriculture and animal husbandry techniques.

Wilding

Cloak Color – Dark green

Motto – "All creatures return to us."

The Temple of the Wildling God deals with management of wild animal populations, forestry, and the protection of ecosystems.

Vintner

Cloak Color – Purple

Motto – "The line between wisdom and madness is one sip."

The Temple of Vintner not only deals with the cultivation of grapes and the production of wine, but they also promote the gathering, cultivation and processing of all medicinal herbs.

Death

Cloak Color – Black

Motto – "For every life, there is a death."

The Temple of Death takes care of the gathering of the dead, the last rites, and disposal of the corpses. They also act as a repository for the last wills and testaments of all citizens.

Characters and Places

QUEENDOM OF ISURRA

ORRIN

Temple of Balance

Chief Justice Anthea – a circuit justice for ten winters until her appointment as Chief Justice of Orrin at the age of thirty winters ("Justice")

Chief Justice Penelope – deceased, predecessor to Anthea as Chief Justice of Orrin

Chief Justice Thalia – deceased, predecessor to Penelope as Chief Justice of Orrin, maternal grandmother to Anthea

Justice Yanaba – junior justice assigned to the city of Orrin after the events of *A Question of Balance*

Justice Erato – junior justice assigned to the circuit of the eastern section of the duchy of Orrin and the southern tip of the duchy of Pana Valley after Anthea is sentenced to the seat of Orrin in "Justice"

Sivan – personal assistant to Chief Justice Anthea and head of the household staff

Donella – senior clerk

Lailani – junior clerk

Chief Warden Little Bear – head of the Balance wardens

Warden Tyra – junior warden, killed in the Battle of Tandor (*A Matter of Death*)

Warden Gina – junior warden

Warden Aglaia – junior warden, died in the battle to retake the Temple of Love (*A Question of Balance*)

Warden Daniel – junior warden

Warden Noko – junior warden

Warden Jonata – junior warden, Aglaia's replacement from the Standora Wardens' Academy, a passive talent

Warden Dezba – junior warden

Warden Tahoma – junior warden

Warden Ahiga – junior warden

Warden Long Feather – junior warden

Warden Ailyn – junior warden, she replaced Tyra after her death

Warden Mylon – junior warden

Hogarth – former chief warden under Justices Thalia and Penelope, now stablemaster, husband of Deborah

Deborah – Head cook, wife of Hogarth

Nathan – squire to Chief Justice Anthea after he was sentenced to pay reparations for stealing bread, an orphan, age ten winters at the time of his sentencing in *A Question of Balance*

Ming Wei – squire to Justice Yanaba, nine winters old at the end of *A Question of Balance*. Originally from Jing, she was sold by her parents to a Jing noble as a sex slave and brought to Issura. When the noble's crimes were discovered, he immolated himself and his slaves. Ming Wei was the only survivor and has severe scar tissue on her face, back and arms.

Temple of Light

High Brother Luc – a circuit priest for twelve winters until his appointment as chief priest at the age of thirty-two winters between the events of "Justice" and "Diplomacy in the Dark"

High Brother Kam – semi-retired, predecessor to Luc as chief priest, poisoned and died during the events of *A Question of Balance*

Brother Mat – Second to Luc. His birth name is Micah. He murdered the real Mat on his way to Orrin from Standora. Died under Anthea's truthspell interrogation in *A Question of Balance*.

Brother Jeremy – youngest junior priest until he is promoted to Luc's second after the events of *A Question of Balance*.

Brother Garbhan – junior priest who is assigned permanently to Orrin after the events of *A Matter of Death*

Istaqa – personal assistant to High Brother Luc and head of the household staff

Edberth – former personal assistant to High Brother Kam, he now acts as evening assistant to High Brother Luc

Henry – stablemaster

Chief Warden Nicholas – head of the Light wardens

Warden Gibb – junior warden, died shortly after the renegades' kidnapping of High Brother Luc in *A Question of Balance*

Warden Mateqai – junior warden, becomes Sister Shi Hua's personal bodyguard during the events of *A Modicum of Truth*

Warden Yar – junior warden

Warden Tadhg – junior warden

Warden Gad – junior warden

Temple of Love

High Sister Gerd – chief priestess, biological daughter of Thalia and Kam, biological mother of Anthea. She was removed from office on charges of fraud, bribery of a public official, unlawful magic, and conspiracy to commit murder. Later, the charges of dealing in demon artifacts and treason were added.

Sister Dragonfly – Gerd's second, *berda* (genderfluid), is acting High Sister after the events in *A Question of Balance*, becomes High Sister after the events in *A Modicum of Truth*

Sister Gretchen – junior priestess, deceased. The discovery of her body in one of Duke Marco's wine barrels precipitates the events in *A Question of Balance*.

Sister Claudia – junior priestess, Dragonfly's second

Sister Shada – junior priestess

Sister Zihna – junior priestess

Sister Ilina – Gerd's second until her death; Lady Katarina DiMara's mother; she died of the wasting disease a year prior to "Justice"

Chief Warden Citana – new chief warden of Love after renegades killed and replaced the entire warden contingent of the temple

Warden Jocasta – junior warden, one of the replacement wardens after the events of *A Question of Balance*

Warden Ekta – junior warden

Gregorios – a eunuch who was High Sister Dragonfly's personal assistant and head of household until their murder prior to the beginning of *A Twist of Love*

Ichik – a eunuch who is Sister Claudia's personal assistant

Iona – Love's maintenance person, she does minor repairs and servicing of the Temple

Temple of Conflict
High Brother Han – chief priest

Brother Piru – junior priest, Han's second

Sister Migina – junior priestess

Brother Yas – junior priest

Temple of Death
High Sister Bertrice – chief priestess

High Brother Kai – deceased, predecessor of Bertrice, retired in Bertrice's favor as the temple seat and became a teaching brother in Standora until his death

Brother Xander – Bertrice's second until her demise during the Battle of Tandor, succeeds her as Orrin's High Brother of Death

Sister Raven Claw – Xander's second when he becomes high brother

Brother Elu – junior priest

Chief Warden Axton – head of the Death wardens

Warden Hitari – junior warden

Temple of Vintner

High Brother Ben – chief priest

Sister Nina – junior priestess

Chief Warden Mangas – head of the Vintner wardens

Warden Golden Eagle – junior warden, murdered by Gerd during the events of *A Twist of Love*

Temple of Mother
High Mother Bianca – chief priestess, she commits suicide when Anthea discovers Bianca has been selling children

High Mother Leocadia – chief priestess, she transferred from the Temple in Gilwas and succeeded Bianca between the events in *A Touch of Mother* and *A Twist of Love*

Chief Warden Maebh – head of the Mother wardens until the events of *A Touch of Mother*

Ademaro – Leocadia's personal chef she brought with her from Gilwas

Temple of Father

High Father Jerrod – chief priest

Temple of Child
High Sister Mya – chief priestess

Brother Turtle – junior priest, helps to save Justice Yanaba by pulling her soul back into her body during the events of *A Modicum of Truth*

Sister Dawn Star – junior priestess

Makawee – Child's head of household and Mya's personal assistant

Chief Warden High Rock – head of the Child wardens

Temple of Wildling

High Brother Jax – chief priest, second form is a wolf

Sister Farrah – Jax's second, second form is a fox

Temple of Thief

High Brother Talbert – chief priest

Sister Cedar Grove – Talbert's second

Brother Teluhci – junior priest

Sister Malila – junior priestess

Chief Warden Sabine – head of the Thief wardens

Temple of Knowledge

High Sister Mariana – chief priestess

Brother Luca – junior priest

Nobility

Duke Benedetto DiMara – father of Marco, Alessa, and Isabella, husband of Cora, convicted of conspiracy to use illegal magic to mind wipe his son Marco during the events of "Justice"; imprisoned at Standora for life.

Lady Cora DiMara – mother of Marco, Alessa, and Isabella, convicted of treason and demon dealing, executed by the Reverend Mother Alara of Balance during the events of "Justice".

Duke Marco DiMara – duke of Orrin, inherited his post at the age of eighteen winters after his parents were found guilty of numerous offenses and stripped of their titles and property

Lady Katarina DiMara (nee' DiLove) – common-born wife of Marco, animal healer. Her mother was Sister Ilina, a priestess of the Temple of Love who died of the wasting sickness the summer before Katarina's eighteenth winter.

Lord Kam DiMara – eldest child of Marco and Katarina and heir to the Duchy of Orrin, named for High Brother Kam of Light, godson of Chief Justice Anthea and High Brother Luc

Lady Alessa DiMara – sister of Marco, a passive talent, lover of Sister Gretchen of Love

Lady Isabella DiMara – sister of Marco, attends the University of Standora

Bartholomew – retainer of Duke Marco's until it was learned he'd assaulted Lady Alessa and Sister Gretchen. Lady Alessa subsequently asked Chief Justice Anthea for clemency and hired him to manage the estates Sister Gretchen had bequeathed to Alessa.

William – retainer of Duke Marco's

Julian – retainer of Duke Marco's

Noemi – a handmaid to Lady Alessa

Arturo – former captain of Duke Marco's flagship. His murder is the precipitating event of "Diplomacy in the Dark".

Titus – captain of Duke Marco's flagship, the *Mars Tranquilus*

Citizens

Malven DiCook – duly elected magistrate of Orrin

Dante – one of Orrin's peacekeepers, dies at the beginning of *A Modicum of Truth*

Barbora – wife of Dante, dies at the beginning of *A Modicum of Truth*

Jaime – one of Orrin's peacekeepers

Leyti – one of Orrin's peacekeepers

Fat Squirrel – one of Orrin's peacekeepers

Drest – a peacekeeper, dismissed by DiCook for extortion

Robin – a peacekeeper, dismissed by DiCook for warning Drest that DiCook was coming to arrest him

Alo – an innkeeper, the owner of the Green Lady Inn near the Embassy District

Xoco – Alo's wife who died giving birth to Chumana

Chumana – Alo's daughter, she is ten winters at the beginning of *A Question of Balance*

Cat and Dog – the leaders of Orrin's street children, Chief Justice Anthea uses them to obtain information outside of the normal Temple intelligence channels

Harold – an Orrin wagoneer

Guilds

Chief Healer Aaron – head of the Healers' Guild

Master Healer Devin – second to Aaron in the Orrin Healer's Guild, originally from New Thenos

Journeywoman Bly – a junior healer, often assists Master Devin at autopsies, later a master healer in her own right

Simi – Bly's apprentice at the Healers Guild when Bly attains master status

Master Healer Una – a master healer who specializes in head trauma and sleep disorders, she also happens to be a dreamwalker

TANDOR

High Brother Dav – chief priest of the Temple of Light

Chief Justice Elizabeth – chief justice of the Temple of Balance

Minerva – the new clerk with the Temple of Balance, a renegade, killed during the fight within the Temple of Balance (*A Modicum of Truth*)

High Brother Aduba – chief priest of the Temple of Conflict

Brother Tighan – second of the Temple of Conflict, a renegade, killed by Aduba during the fall of Tandor

High Brother Nantan – chief priest of the Temple of Death

Sister Reby – second of the Temple of the Wildling God, first introduced as a shapeshifting thief in "The Perfect Partner", second form is a polecat

Brother Sisquoc – priest of the Temple of the Wildling God, second form is a panther

Brother Trajan – priest of the Temple of the Wilding God, second form is a wolf

Sister Jumping Mouse – priestess of the Temple of the Wildling God, second form is a kangaroo rat

Duke Enzo DiToscana – Duke of Tandor, murdered by a skinwalker possessing his wife

Duchess Nadine DiToscana – the widow of Duke Enzo of Tandor

Ural DiSand – merchant from Tandor, implicated in the Assassin Guild plots in Orrin, killed while possessed by a skinwalker (*A Modicum of Truth*)

Amarantha DiRoma – Tandoran merchant, rival of Ural DiSand, murdered by renegades shortly before they poisoned most of the personnel of the Tandoran Temples

Govind – a silversmith who assisted with the defense of Tandor against the demon army, settled in Orrin after the evacuation and fall of Tandor

The Wave Dancer – Duchess Nadine of Tandor's flagship, one of two remaining ships in Tandor prior to the Battle of Tandor

STANDORA – capital city of Issura

Reverend Mother Alara – head of Issura's Temple of Balance

Justice Rose – novice training priestess of the main Temple of Balance in Standora when Anthea was a novice

Justice Melanippe – a novice in Anthea's class. She was the top student, but she was also recruited by Thief to report on any wrongdoing in Balance.

Reverend Father Farrell – head of Issura's Temple of Light

Brother Elroy – a Light priest, aide to Reverend Father Farrell, and a distance speaker who accompanies the Isurran and Sea Peoples fleets to Tandor in *A Matter of Death*

Brother Long Wind – a Light priest and aide to Reverend Father Farrell; he accompanies the queen's army to Tandor in *A Matter of Death*

Brother Garbhan – a Light priest and aide to Reverend Father Farrell; he remains in Orrin during and after the events of *A Matter of Death*

Brother Jon – novice training priest at the main Temple of Light in Standora, murdered by the skinwalker at Samael DiRoy's abandoned manse prior to *A Question of Balance*

High Sister Imala – a Love priestess, considered to be the lead contender for position of Reverend Mother of Love; she accompanies the queen's army in A Matter of Death

Chief Warden Catherine – Imala's chief warden; she was a classmate of Mateqai's at the Warden Academy and the two had a physical relationship

Warden Hototo – a junior Love warden

Reverend Father Grey Shadow – head of Issura's Temple of Thief

Brother White Wolf – a senior priest of Thief; he's a personal friend of High Sister Imala

Queen Teodora – reigning monarch of Issura

Crown Princess Chiara – eldest child and heir of Queen Teodora of Issura; lady general of the queen's army

Duke White Eagle – former Conflict brother, left the order to marry Crown Princess Chiara; honorary title Duke of Standora as the future queen's consort; lord general of the queen's army

PANA VALLEY

Lord Aleister DeGrove – noble noted for his vineyards

JING EMPIRE

CHENGZHOU

Empress Bao De – ruler of Jing a century before Bao Yu, she sacrificed herself to stop a demon army

Empress Bao Yu – ruler of Jing until her death from natural causes during "Courting Trouble"

Emperor Bao Chengwu – current ruler of Jing, succeeded his mother Bao Yu during "Courting Trouble"

Ambassador Quan Po – half-brother of the current Jing emperor Bao Chengwu; was heir to the throne until his nephew was born

Reverend Father Jin – head of Jing's Temple of Light

Sister Shi Hua – a priestess of Light, who was tapped as Po's bodyguard. She received additional training from Conflict, Thief, and Love. Originally from the town of Yintze in the southern province of Chu.

Brother Lin – novice master of Light

Brother Jian – a priest of Light, classmate of Shi Hua during their novice years

Brother Fa – a Wildling priest, his second form is a tiger, a friend of Shi Hua and Jian during their novice years

Justice Mei Wen – a priestess of Balance, Shi Hua's closest friend other than Jian during their novice years

Sister Yin Li – a priestess of Love, Shi Hua's maternal aunt

Yin Shang – the son of Sister Yin Li and Brother Shang

Reverend Father Chen – head of Jing's Temple of Conflict

Brother Shang – a priest of Conflict, Shi Hua's instructor when she was a novice

Reverend Father Biming – head of Jing's Temple of Thief

The Unbridled – a spy ship used by the Temple of Thief, a four-masted carrack built in the Iberian duchy of Valencia, captained by Reverend Father Biming during *A Modicum of Truth*

Brother Hadar – a priest of Thief from the Kingdom of Hejaz, serving on board *The Unbridled*

ISLANDS OF THE SEA PEOPLES

Kingdom of O'ahu

Prince Alika – youngest son of the king of the Sea Peoples, one of Sister Gretchen's worshippers, the father of her unborn child

Captain Iakepa – senior captain of the O'ahu trading fleet

DINÉ NATION

AJÉÍ (HEART)

Temple of Balance

Reverend Mother Hózhó – head of the Diné Temple of Balance

Justice Mosi – a junior justice

Justice Spotted Fawn – the western circuit justice for the Diné Nation, killed in the Battle of Tandor

Bidzii – Spotted Fawn's clerk, he was fluent in Issuran so the justice spoke through him; killed in the Battle of Tandor

Temple of Light

Brother Bumblebee – junior priest of Light with the Diné army, Anthea's half-brother by her father Kilchii

Temple of Conflict

Reverend Father Kilchii – head of the Diné Temple of Conflict. When he first met Anthea, he gave his name as "Nizhé'é", which in the Diné language means "your father" because he is her biological father.

Temple of Knowledge

Sister Lizard – junior priestess with the Diné army at Tandor

Temple of Thief

Sister Shideezhi – junior priestess, Anthea's half-sister by their father Kilchii

Temple of Wildling

Sister Cheona – junior priestess, her second form is a panther

Elders

Matriarch Nascha – elected leader of the Diné Nation, a clan elder

Elder Johona – a clan elder

Elder Chooli – a clan elder who was murdered to fuel the hatching of a demon egg

Citizens

Niyol – Nacha's eldest brother

Sike – Johona's eldest brother

Tibah – deceased, Chief Justice Thalia's mother, Reverend Mother Hózhó and Matriarch Nascha's great-aunt, and Chief Justice Anthea's great-grandmother

CLIFFDWELLERS

Healer Kotori – a physician with the Diné army during the siege of Tandor

PLAINS NATIONS – **COMANCHE**

High Brother Pecos – a senior Conflict priest with the Diné army during the siege of Tandor

Acknowledgments

As always, much love and gratitude to Elaina Lee and Jaye Manus. I couldn't do this without you two.

To Bella the Princess Pup for making me walk away from my desk once in a while for a constitutional and play time.

To my son, his significant other, my brand new grandson, and their three fur babies, I love you all.

To my Darling Husband who kept me in ice cream and pizza and dealt with the disaster of water in the basement while I finished this book. Thank you, thank you, thank you!

And last, but not least, to the readers who insisted they needed more of Anthea and Luc. Thank you so much for reading these stories!

Suzan Harden transitioned from writing information technology manuals for companies and legal articles for a law enforcement magazine to her first love, fantasy and science fiction in all their forms. She's the author of the Bloodlines, the 888-555-HERO, and the Justice series.